At the stroke of eight, in walked Bo Deaver.

One or two of the girls almost gasped. Hardly anyone had seen the easygoing basketball player in a blazer and pressed slacks before. He was handsome as a movie star and seemed bigger than life.

Ellen whispered feverishly into Crystal's ear. "Exactly on the dot. Wow! You sure know how to train your men!"

Crystal calmly brushed a few fallen crumbs from her billowing lace evening dress and waited for Bo to approach.

"Hi, gorgeous," he called when he was still fifteen feet or so away. "Ready to go?"

Crystal was taking her time as she started to rise but he swept right past her... and moved down the line to Donna's chair.

"Well, you're a little early," said Donna, "but I guess so."

Bo turned to Crystal. "Hi, Crystal, how're you doing?"

Crystal didn't answer. Her face was bright red. And as Bo looked away, Sabra whispered furiously into her ear, "I'll get even for you, Crystal! I swear I will!"

Other Avon Books in the
GOING FOR IT *series*

BALANCING ACT
by Rebecca Larsen

Coming soon

SUMMER DREAMS
by Bill Gutman

OUT OF CONTROL
by Sam Bittman

BAREBACK
by Merrilee Steiner

THIN ICE
by E. M. Rees

Avon Books are available at special quantity discounts for bulk purchases for sales promotions, premiums, fund raising or educational use. Special books, or book excerpts, can also be created to fit specific needs.

For details write or telephone the office of the Director of Special Markets, Avon Books, Dept. FP, 1790 Broadway, New York, New York 10019, 212-399-1357. *IN CANADA:* Director of Special Sales, Avon Books of Canada, Suite 210, 2061 McCowan Rd., Scarborough, Ontario M1S 3Y6, 416-293-9404.

Making Waves
A.C. CHANDLER

AN AVON FLARE BOOK

GOING FOR IT #1—MAKING WAVES is an original publication of Avon Books. This work has never before appeared in book form.

AVON BOOKS
A division of
The Hearst Corporation
1790 Broadway
New York, New York 10019

Copyright © 1985 by Cloverdale Press/Jeffrey Weiss Group
Published by arrangement with Cloverdale Press/Jeffrey Weiss Group
Library of Congress Catalog Card Number: 85-90657
ISBN: 0-380-89899-3

All rights reserved, which includes the right to
reproduce this book or portions thereof in any form
whatsoever except as provided by the U.S. Copyright Law.
For information address Cloverdale Press,
133 Fifth Avenue, New York, New York 10003.

First Flare Printing, November 1985

AVON TRADEMARK REG. U. S. PAT. OFF. AND IN
OTHER COUNTRIES, MARCA REGISTRADA, HECHO EN
U.S.A.

Printed in the U.S.A.

WFH 10 9 8 7 6 5 4 3 2 1

Making Waves

Chapter One

Donna Wilder had heard about "burnout." Was that what she was going through right now? All she knew was, that morning, as the team's bus rolled along, she just didn't care about the swim meet. She didn't even care that if she won her events in the sectionals today, she'd go on to compete for the New York State championships.

Gregory and Bret—her boyfriend and her brother—were on her mind. She felt as though they were pulling her in two different directions, and as she sat there staring dully out the window, her thoughts drifted back to yesterday's quarrel. It had started with Greg sitting like a lump through the first act of the Platterkill Players' performance of *Three Men on a Horse*. The play was so funny. The audience was roaring, but Greg hadn't even cracked a smile.

"You don't like the show, man?" Bret had asked, leaning past Donna during intermission. He was only trying to be friendly.

"Yeah, it's okay," Gregory had answered him moodily.

"So, what's the problem?"

"You really want to know?"

Bret gave him a shrewd look. "I bet I know already."

Gregory let out a sigh that was like a teakettle boiling over, and he actually seemed to jump in his seat. "Look, I like you, I really do, but the thing is—I hardly ever see Donna as it is—"

"Hey!" Donna protested, but they kept right on talking, as though she weren't even there.

"You want me to sit somewhere else? I mean, I bought the tickets, but that's okay...."

"No, forget it. I just want to watch the play in peace."

"Suit yourself." And they both plunked back down in their seats.

After that, Donna couldn't enjoy the rest of the play. What was going on onstage just seemed like meaningless words flying by—and people laughing and laughing. When it was over and they rose with the rest of the crowd and pressed out into the aisle, Donna didn't even have a chance to try to make peace between Bret and Gregory. Mumbling something about having work to do, Gregory gave her a quick kiss and stalked out of the theater.

Bret was puzzled. "What's his problem, anyway? We planned this thing three weeks ago."

"No, Bret, *you* planned it."

"Well, I thought it would be a good way for you to relax the night before the sectionals."

"The meet is no big deal, Bret. But my relationship with Greg *is*."

"You never know," said Bret with a mysterious wink, "what might be a big deal and what might not."

But Donna didn't pay any attention. Her thoughts were on Gregory. The moment she got home, she called him. "Can we talk about this?" she had said.

"I guess so." He sounded more weary than grumpy.

"I think you hurt Bret's feelings."

"Yeah, well, I'm sorry. I'll apologize the next time I see him."

"Maybe it's me you should be mad at."

"Maybe. You *could* say no once in a while, you know, when he keeps bugging you about all that extra practicing. It's ridiculous, anyway. You're already winning all your races hands down. And he's not even the coach!"

"Look, the meet will be over tomorrow. After that, we'll have a lot of time together."

"Yeah, sure. Until the *next* one." Donna waited. Greg had fallen into a long silence, and all she heard now was his breathing. Suddenly he was back. "And what gets me is that I don't even think you like it that much."

"I *do* like it...." She had meant that to sound stronger than it had.

"You know something? I don't think you even know *what* you like."

Now she was feeling confused. She hated that. "I know I like *you*, Greg. Are you going to come to see me swim tomorrow?"

"Yeah, if I can get a hitch."

"Don't hitch. You could drive down with Bret and my parents."

"I'll get there on my own. I promise."

"Great!" But she hadn't really felt all that great when she got off the phone. And she was still feeling down when she got up the next morning.

"We're here," the coach called out, and Donna snapped back to the present. The words carved into the stone archway on her right read LEELAND COLLEGE. The bus turned through the gates and rolled along the tree-shaded campus until it came to a halt behind a line of other buses. Donna's team was one of twelve that were competing in the meet. Leeland College wasn't all that close to any of them, but it was the only place within reach with a fifty-meter pool.

She was dazzled by her first sight of the pool, sparkling blue under the glassed-in roof. She thought about what her brother had said in his deepest frustration: "How am I going to get you to the Nationals, let alone the Olympics, if you don't have a regulation-size pool to train in?" It was true. The faster her times got, the dinkier the Platterkill pool seemed.

The Olympics! It sounded so glamorous, but was that really what she wanted? And even if she did give it her best shot, what chance did she honestly have? But Bret was so determined. It meant so much to him!

By the time she'd gotten into her swimsuit and joined her team at the pool, there were already a lot of other swimmers splashing around in it, doing their warm-ups. Not much room, she told herself, to do anything more than get wet and practice a few strokes. So she slipped in the aquamarine water, made a few stabs at practicing, then climbed out again and contented herself with stretches on the mats next to the pool.

She was still at it when, at ten o'clock, the starter's gun went off for the first race of the meet. It was a relay. Donna had hoped to be in it because she would have liked, for a change, to swim with three of her friends instead of all by herself. But the coach had said no, wanting to save his star for better things.

Another team took the relay, but then came the 200-meter freestyle. It was one of Donna's best events; that is, if she was in the mood. She went over to the side of the pool to watch the first heat of the race, which would pit the six slowest-rated swimmers against one another. For the third or fourth time she also glanced across the pool at the benches where the spectators sat. Once more her parents waved to her, and Bret gave her a thumbs-up sign. She looked all around the pool room. Still no sign of Gregory.

After the first heat there were five more before Donna and the other fastest swimmers stepped up to the blocks. "Don't worry about winning," Bret had said. "You're going to do that, anyway. Use whatever starting dive you're feeling most up to at the moment. But hit the water far out and fast, and go all out for times.

I want to see you lob at least fifteen seconds off anything you've ever done before—even in your dreams. Knock their socks off, Do-Do!"

"Swimmers, take your marks!" boomed the starter's voice. This was no time to be looking up, but she took one last glance to see if Gregory was there. He wasn't. She felt the heart go out of her just as the starter's gun went off.

The five other swimmers hit the water ahead of her. She didn't have to look up to know that the eager smile had suddenly fallen from her brother's face, which now wore a look of astonishment.

I can't let him down! I can't! she told herself. Not her brother—who counted on her so.

The strength that Bret's relentless training had pumped into her arms and legs now exploded into a powerful stroke. The streamlining positions he'd coached her so hard in made her body become one with the water, cut down its resistance to her—and she sliced through the pool like a knife through butter. With every fraction of a second she gained on the field. By the end of the first lap she was almost even with the lead swimmer. By the middle of the second she had pulled well ahead of the girl. By the third lap she was out in the open. At the end of the pool she went into her flip turn, knowing that Bret was sending his message from out there: "Sprint! Sprint! Pour it on!"

When she emerged from the water victorious, he was on his feet. Her parents were on their feet. That was nice to see, but what was the big deal? she asked herself. After all, the race wasn't over. She still had to go up against the winners of the other heats. But just then, the starter announced a new all-time state record! And from the far end of the place, two hands clenched together high over someone's head. It was a victory sign. Gregory was there, telling her, himself, and everyone in sight that his girlfriend was a champion.

Donna didn't best her own time in the finals, but she won the race without any trouble. It almost looked as though the other swimmers had lost their taste for competing. She also swept the 100-meter individual medley, though it was back to back with the first race. Later she went on to win the 100-meter butterfly. It was her day, and everyone let her know it.

Then the bomb fell.

"I want you to meet someone," Bret said, leading her over to a bench where a quiet-looking man of twenty-five or so sat patiently waiting. "This man is the reason why I told you that you never know what a big deal is until it smacks you with a towel. Meet Stanislaw Worshak."

"Hello."

"How do you do," said the man, pronouncing his words very carefully so that he could be understood despite his thick European accent.

"Do you know who he is? Do you recognize his name?" her brother asked in a low voice.

"I . . . I think I've heard it."

"He held three world's records before he left his country to come here. This is the man who would have beaten me—*maybe*—if we'd both made it to the Olympics. But they kept him out because of the boycott. And me, I had that stupid accident that botched up my knee for good!" The intense look of pain that passed over Bret's face passed quickly, like a cloud from in front of the sun. His glow came back. "But that's all water under the diving board—and Stany here's got something to tell you."

To Donna, Worshak seemed a little bit shy, like her. His voice was as soft as his smile as he said, "I think you are a wonderful swimmer. Very good possibilities. Your brother has brought me out from Colorado—and now I'm glad."

"Colorado?"

"Yes, I'm ... scout ... for that high school just been started up two years ago."

"Olympic High?"

"Yes, of course. You have heard?"

"Everyone's heard of it—"

"He wants you to go there," Bret broke in, his voice almost trembling with held-back excitement. "A full scholarship!"

"We don't guarantee everyone at school make Olympics. Many will not. Most. But everyone gets the chance for best training. Doc Stimpson's best swimming coach in this country, maybe world. I know—I have seen all."

Bret was glowing. "What do you say, Do-Do?"

Donna's eyes were riveted on Gregory, who had quietly followed them and was now standing not five feet away, listening. The expression on his face seemed to say that he knew what her answer would be, that he felt he had already lost her.

Worshak may have been a little deficient in English, but there was nothing wrong with his eyes. They moved rapidly from Donna, to the boy, then back again to rest gently on her. "Big decisions not always easy. She needs time to think."

Bret was too enthusiastic to be patient. "This is the most fantastic opportunity of your life, kiddo. I only wish they had had a school like this when I was starting to compete. By the time that accident clobbered me, I might already have had a few championships to look back on. Donna, you never know what might happen down the road. Take your best shot while you've got the chance."

Donna's parents, who were also standing by, had developed a knack for remaining silent, particularly when one of their children was at center stage. But Mrs. Wilder was also a born diplomat and tension breaker. "For goodness sake, Bret. Donna hasn't said she doesn't want to go. All this happened just two seconds ago. Give the poor girl a chance to breathe!" She clapped her hands together. "Listen, everybody, it's training-breaking time. Fattening, oily, greasy, delicious foods are beckoning. We're all going out for nothing less than pizza—with everything on it. You, too, Mr. Worshak."

The scout stood up. "No, thank you. I make report." He quickly jotted something down on a piece of paper and handed it to Donna. "My telephone number at motel. You call me later.

Maybe tomorrow. I'm here to eight P.M. We talk, eh? Whatever you decide, good to meet you."

Donna had a hurried private conversation with Gregory. He'd managed to borrow his father's car—which was a rare feat—and was in no mood to be in the midst of the entire Wilder family just now. Donna begged off her mother's invitation and insisted on driving back to Platterkill with Greg. She knew he was hurting.

"Listen, Greg," she said as they sped along. "There's nothing to be upset about. I'm not going there."

"That's what you say, but I don't believe it."

"What do you mean?"

"You'll do anything your brother wants you to do."

"That's not true."

"Look, I don't want to talk about it."

They drove for half an hour, lost in their own thoughts. He pulled up to her house and stopped the car. "I thought we'd go eat somewhere," she said.

"I'm just not hungry."

They sat in silence for another five minutes. "I think you're being unfair to me."

"Look, I know you have a big talent. And I don't want to stand in your way."

"That's not what I meant."

"Well, whatever you meant, I'm sorry."

"I mean, you don't trust me. You think I'm going to go to Olympic High and we'll break up."

"I just don't think you have any choice at all. You feel too sorry for Bret! And I don't know *why*. There's nothing wrong with him except that he can't race anymore. So what? I mean, I'm sorry, too, but it's not the end of the world."

"Please don't talk about him that way."

"I wouldn't have to if he wasn't milking that failed-sports-hero bit so he can wind you around his little finger."

"That's not true," she said, growing very agitated. "He doesn't try to do that at all. And even if I did go—"

"See what I mean?"

"Gregory, I don't *hate* swimming—no matter what you seem to think!"

"But you don't know if you love it, either, do you?"

"Look. Give me a break! I can't answer all these questions. But this *is* a chance to accomplish something, isn't it?"

He twisted around in his seat. "First you tell me, 'Don't worry, I'm not going.' Then you tell me, 'This is a chance to accomplish something!' You're contradicting yourself!"

"What about *you?* You said that you wouldn't want to stand in my way!"

He gazed at her with surprise. "When did I say that?"

"Just a few minutes ago!"

Gregory took a deep breath. "Like, you know—that's the male, macho thing that I'm *supposed* to say. Look at me, folks, the heroic guy who steps aside. And maybe I *would* if I thought that was what you really wanted."

She blew up. "Everybody seems to think they can make up my mind for me!"

"Maybe that's because you don't seem to be doing it for yourself."

"Well, I will!" She bolted out of the car.

"What are you angry at *me* for?"

"Because I *want* to be!" She slammed the door and dashed into the house.

That outburst, of course, didn't solve her problem. She was up most of the night and on edge all the next day. She spent most of it—a Sunday—avoiding talking to Bret and hanging up before she finished dialing Gregory's number.

When evening came, she still didn't know what she wanted to do. Gregory was only a part of it—a big part, certainly—but there was more. Donna had a lot of friends in Platterkill, the only town she'd ever lived in. She'd miss her family, too, if she went so far away. They had always been together. Even Bret, who was in his mid-twenties and very grown-up, lived only two blocks away. And, though she was a little ashamed to admit it, she was devoted to her bedroom with its canopy bed and all the dolls she'd ever owned still neatly tucked away in one of her closets.

And Colorado was—where? She pulled out a map and tried to work out the distance with a tape measure. Maybe two thousand five hundred miles away!

Then what about all that training she'd have to go through? Much more, probably, than she had to put up with here. What an awesome change for a long-shot chance of making the

Olympics! And how good a long shot was it, really, when there were so many other great swimmers around—people from out West, such as Crystal Delehanty, the "Golden Girl."

She looked at the clock for the tenth time that evening. It was seven-fifteen already, and Mr. Worshak would be leaving at eight. What should she do?

Suddenly the telephone rang. It seemed so loud that it made her jump. And with an eerie feeling that it was the scout from Olympic High calling for a final decision, she picked it up. "Hello?" she asked cautiously.

"I've been thinking it over." It was Gregory.

"Yes?"

"And—you know—like, I care about you."

Her heart melted. "I care about you, too, Greg."

"What I'm trying to say is, I don't want to see you going through this being torn in half stuff because of me. So ... uh ... look. If you want to go, don't get all worried about me. I mean, you're going to be here through the summer, right? Then you'll be back for Christmas. And in between we'll put our parents' telephone bills into orbit."

"Greg, I love you!" she blurted out wildly.

"You don't have to go *that* far!"

"I mean it!"

"Okay, go that far."

As soon as they hung up she telephoned Stanislaw Worshak to tell him that she accepted the offer.

Chapter Two

But there was no such thing as a summer vacation at Olympic High. Two weeks after Donna's spring term ended in Platterkill, she was on her way to Colorado. Gregory, who had come over to help her pack, looked very unhappy when he kissed her good-bye. Her parents got misty-eyed themselves as they gave her farewell hugs. Bret drove her the thirty miles to the airport, where she took a night flight for Chicago. Then, after a two-hour layover at O'Hare Airport, she hopped another plane from Chicago to Denver. And finally she climbed onto a bus. The bus ride took as long as any of the plane trips. If she hadn't fallen into a dazed half-sleep along the way, she might have enjoyed watching the morning sun come up over the peaks of the Rockies.

At long last the bus took a turn off the main road and began a winding climb, which made her dizzy, even in her half-asleep state. She untangled her limbs from her bunched-up sprawl across two seats, rubbed her eyes, and looked out.

Donna's first sight ever of the legendary Olympic High made her gasp.

The parts of it—and the whole of it together—were beautiful. The campus comprised a wide circle of buildings and playing fields surrounding a vast, stretching plain. In the far distance high mountain peaks reached up into the clouds—and on one summit into summertime snow.

The buildings were gracefully designed, made of beautiful, dark-stained wood, many of them with high, sloping roofs, like ski lodges. Others, which must have been training areas, were large and oval. A lot of the buildings had white trim around the windows with little boxes at sill level from which brightly colored geraniums and petunias spilled. There were flower gardens, too, which had been planted around all the buildings, and these were shaded by stately aspen trees and evergreens. A little farther out were the basketball courts, running tracks, and practice fields for every Olympic sport. At the outer edge of the circle, moving off toward the mountains, were the corrals, grazing lands, and stables of the riding squad.

With growing excitement Donna searched for the outdoor pool. She found it in front of one of the largest of the bread-loaf-shaped buildings. The Mark Spitz Pavilion! The thrill she felt was electric and ran up her spine.

She had read in sports magazines that some of the greatest swimmers in America would soon be coming out of Olympic High. And Donna Wilder would be among them!

The bus let her off in front of the Academic Studies Building, before it rolled on. It was here where the letter she held tightly in her hand told her to report. She found the office of the Dean of Admissions and went inside. An assistant led her right away to Margaret Nolan, a woman around fifty who greeted Donna with a strong handshake and a kindly smile.

After a little friendly, get-acquainted conversation, Mrs. Nolan got down to business. "Your grades were quite good at Platterkill High School, and we expect you to keep up the good work through your junior and senior years here. We consider academics very important, and we don't cut any corners on them. A student might be the best athlete in the school—or even in the world—but it still wouldn't matter. She or he will be suspended from training if any of the grades fall below passing—and dropped altogether if they stay that way.

"What we *do* have, though," she went on, "is a compact schedule for your classes to allow you more time to train. They don't begin until ten-thirty. And they end at two P.M. Homework is probably best done in the evenings after training and dinner. And, Donna, since it's essential that you get enough sleep to be able to handle the pace we keep up here, we have a ten o'clock lights-out policy in the dorms. Saturday nights it's eleven-thirty." She paused briefly. "Is there anything you want to ask me, Donna?"

"Have most of your students been here since their freshman year?"

"Yes. A few of them transferred in after a year or two elsewhere, like you. But we don't take anyone after that." She saw the line of worry on Donna's face. "Don't worry. If there's anything you're behind in, we'll give you time to catch up."

That wasn't what Donna had in mind, but she was too embarrassed to say anything. Suddenly Mrs. Nolan guessed what was bothering her. "Oh, Donna, I wouldn't worry about making friends, even if you are a latecomer. People are very open here. Remember, they've all left their homes far behind, and they're as eager as you are to make new connections. And, please, if you have any problems of any kind at all, do come and see me. That's what I'm here for."

The dean leaned forward in her chair. "Now you'll want to get settled. I'm putting you into a room with Margaret Whimsey. I'm afraid she's not on the swim squad, though most of the swimmers do bunch together, but their rooms are already taken. Do you mind?"

"No, that's all right," Donna replied uncertainly. She didn't know why, but she was beginning to feel shaky again.

Mrs. Nolan started to rise. "Would you like to go there now and settle in? I'm sure you must be very tired. Or would you rather go see Coach Stimpson first? He's looking forward to having a little talk with you."

"I . . . I think I'd like to meet him, but . . ." She cast a weary glance at the duffel bag and the heavy suitcase she'd dropped in one corner of the office. They had been such a drag for the whole trip.

"You can leave your luggage here. I'll have someone put your bags in your room. It's number twenty-one."

Donna perked up. "Thank you very much—for everything."

"My pleasure. Shall I show you how to get to the swimming building?"

"Isn't it the one next to the outside pool?"

"That's the one." She gave Donna another handshake, and Olympic High's newest swimmer went out into the sunshine.

The sign in the entranceway said that the head coach's office was one flight up. Donna mounted the stairs to the landing, then walked down the narrow corridor until she came to a door with Coach Stimpson's name on it. Had she been a little more alert, she would have noticed another door right next to it marked ENTER HERE. Instead she pushed through the first door and broke right in on a conversation.

Doc Stimpson was sitting behind a desk in front of the far wall, which was made of glass. It overlooked the pool area one flight below. As Donna entered, the girl who was sitting dripping wet in the chair facing him turned around with startled eyes. Stimpson looked up, as did a younger, muscular man seated in a side chair with his arms folded over his chest.

"You're the new team member?" the head coach asked.

"Yes, sir."

"Would you mind stepping outside for a few minutes? There's a little waiting room just over there, through that door." He pointed off to his right.

Donna was flustered. She now realized that she should have gone into that room first. And it was dumb of her not to have knocked. Feeling stupid, she nodded quickly and walked through the door.

The waiting room had a glass wall of its own. Set in it was a glass door that led out to a little landing and a stairway that went down to the pool area. Having nothing better to do, she stepped out onto the landing and gazed down over the railing.

Her heart practically thumped to a stop. Coming out of the water was a figure who could have stepped right off a cover of *Swimming World* magazine. At least, Donna was pretty sure she recognized her. As soon as the girl pulled off her cap and shook loose her mane of shimmering golden hair, Donna knew without a doubt that it was the "Golden Girl" herself—Crystal Delehanty! Fascinated, she watched Delehanty walk across the deck with the kind of easy stride that seemed to bespeak the fact that this bronze-skinned, tawny beauty simply owned the place.

Donna had never been a jealous or envious person. Nevertheless, for some reason, she found the sight of Crystal Delehanty in person upsetting and threatening. Turning, she went back into the waiting room.

"Well, Sabra—" It was Doc Stimpson's voice

coming through a crack in the door, which had swung just the slightest bit open. "I wish I could agree with you and say that time is going to take care of it. But the truth is that the training program is just not working for you."

"But, Doc, I've been trying so hard."

"I know that. I know. You've put in two hard years here. *No one* has worked harder than you. But the truth is, you're just not coming along the way you should be for the amount of effort you've expended."

"Well, I know there are things I could be doing to improve my technique—"

"Sabra, that's just why I've held on to you this long. Because I see that you're working your heart out. And, believe me, I'm the last one to say that with your kind of dedication miracles can't happen. But there are certain limitations that people are born with. Your body—"

"I'm working on my body, Doc! I'm lifting weights. I'm running with the track team. I'm using the Nautilus and the Universals. And I'm taking extra protein with my—"

"I think that's pushing it too hard," he said softly. "I like my swimmers to do most of their workouts in the water."

"I'm in the water more than anyone else!"

"I'm aware of that too. And I know that you've been getting a lot of extra coaching from Jim here. But that's just it. This is all very costly to us—even more in terms of energy than money. And with new students coming in all the time I'm afraid that you're just going to have to give way...."

Donna had been standing outside, listening. She knew she should not be eavesdropping, but that poor girl's desperation had gotten to her. It churned up her own doubts. Here was someone who so badly wanted to be kept on. And the coach was as much as saying that new students, like Donna—who wasn't even sure why she had come here—were pushing her out! She felt horrible.

"I don't have to be a champion," the girl in the office was pleading. "If I can just stay on and be a part of it all. I can train for the relays. I can—"

"Hold it." There was a long silence, except for the heavy sigh that Donna could hear coming through the door. "All right," said the coach, not sounding at all happy about it. "We'll give it one more shot. But you'll have to show some real improvement very soon."

"Thank you, Doc! Thank you, Jim!"

"This is only a probation," Coach Stimpson reminded her.

"I know! I know! But I'm going to surprise you! I really am!"

"I hope so."

"Just wait and see how good I can be!"

The door to the waiting room was flung open, and Sabra Siebel lurched through it, more or less backward. Donna was so happy for her that she wanted to flash a smile. But the look on the other girl's face made her smile freeze in place. This was the look of someone who knew she was face-to-face with her future. It was a gaze of fear, and of something more—maybe hatred. With another quick, jerky movement the girl spun away from Donna, pushed through the glass door, and hurried down the steps to the pool.

Donna felt so shaken that she didn't hear Doc Stimpson calling to her to come in. He was standing at the door now, repeating her name. She followed him inside.

"You'd better take another chair," the coach said, returning to his desk. "That one's a bit damp."

Her mind still a bit numb, Donna stood there without moving. The man named Jim unfolded his arms and brought over a chair from the other side of the room.

"Uh . . . thank you."

"This is my assistant coach for the women swimmers, Jim Sileki."

"Hi," he said with a brisk little smile that curled up his thin black moustache. "I'm the one who's going to make your life miserable."

"Don't hate him for it, though," Doc Stimpson said, chuckling. "It's his job to be the bad guy. That makes me the good guy . . . provided everyone does her job." He took out his glasses, put them on, and reached into his desk. "Let me get your report here. Ah, yes. I have this letter from your coach at Platterkill High School. And another from the coach of the YWCA near you. And here's one from your brother." He looked up. "How is Bret, by the way?"

28

"He's okay," Donna replied.

"Your brother was a very good swimmer. I remember him. It was just too bad about his knee injury. Couldn't they fix that?"

"He walks fine. But he can't use the leg right in swimming. Bret went to a lot of doctors, and they all gave up. Now he says it doesn't matter much because he's too old to compete."

"Yes. It really was a shame, wasn't it, Jim?"

Jim nodded.

"He could have gone all the way, in my opinion." Stimpson stopped to pull his left earlobe. It must be a habit, Donna thought; she had seen him doing it when she barged into the office the first time.

"Well, anyway," the coach went on, "according to your report, you are a remarkable young lady. You do well in all strokes, which is very rare in itself. And you have impressive times." He studied her for a moment. "Am I making you nervous?"

"No!" she said. "It's just all the excitement, I guess."

"How long have you been swimming?"

"Well, our whole family's been doing it for as long as I can remember. But my parents aren't so much into it anymore."

"They got tired of it?"

"No—I don't know. . . . Well, maybe it had something to do with Bret's accident. Everybody got very depressed. . . ."

"What about you? You still like it, anyway?"

"Sure," she said. But there had been just the slightest hesitation before she replied.

The coach pulled his earlobe again. For some reason the habit bothered her.

Now Doc Stimpson's tone of voice changed slightly as he leaned back in his chair. "Why did you want to come here?"

"I . . . uh . . . I want to be the best swimmer I can be."

"You know that all our people are Olympic hopefuls. Do you want to make the Olympics and win there?"

"Yes, sir."

"I'm asking this because, more than anything, an athlete has to really want it. You can have all the technique and power and stamina in the world. But if you don't want it—if you don't want to win more than anything else in the world—you won't have what it takes to reach down for that extra something in yourself. Somebody will beat you out in the end."

"Yes," she said very softly, perhaps a bit too softly. "I . . . understand that."

He studied her for a moment. "You know, it's always best to get things out in the open right at the beginning. Are there any problems you feel you have? Any at all?"

He was staring at her so hard that Donna thought she'd better give him one. *Any* problem except the fact that she felt so confused. "Well," she said slowly, "I'm not all that good at distance swimming."

"Not good?" He smiled. "Or you don't care for it?"

This man, she realized, was very smart. She had the feeling he was looking right through her. "I guess I don't care for it."

"No problem, that's not a big thing here. We mostly use distance practice for strengthening our swimmers for the middle and sprint events. Except for a couple of people on the team, we don't stress speed in distance. That's because at this school we don't concentrate on the whole sport of swimming, just on what it takes to win events at the Nationals and the Olympics. So we leave out the utility strokes, too. Donna, is there anything else on your mind? Anything you want to tell me?"

"No, sir."

"Stanislaw—Mr. Worshak—says in his report that there was some holding back on your part before you accepted the invitation to come here. You want to tell me anything about that?" He was giving her another one of those looks.

"N-no, sir," she began with a stammer. "I just didn't expect it, that's all. And it ... it took time to really ..." Her voice trailed off.

"Well, I guess that's as good an explanation as any," he said quickly as he closed the file and tucked it out of sight. "Don't mind us. We always give our new people the third degree." He beamed a warm smile, stood up, and offered her his hand. "Welcome to Olympic High!"

Donna felt relieved. She turned to the assistant coach. Sileki tilted his head and lifted his eyebrows in what was probably his version of a smile.

"I'm sure," Doc Stimpson went on, "that you

must be interested in meeting the rest of the squad, so why don't you go down to the pool area and introduce yourself."

"Yes, I will." She thanked him and left.

Standing by the glass wall, the head coach watched her descend the steps. "Something about this kid bothers me, Jim. From what I read about her she's tremendous, a natural . . . real potential. But something's missing there, and it could make all the difference."

"Will to win?"

"Well, she wins back at her home meets." He turned away from the window. "But maybe her brother is her inspiration back there. I tell you, what I feel in my gut is that we've got *two* motivation problems in this school now, instead of one. This kid isn't really sure she even wanted to come here. And Miss Wonderful down there—our Golden Girl—she's forgotten why she came. Frankly, Jim, I was hoping that you'd have Crystal really burning up the pool by now. But it seems that while I was away with the Olympic Committee she's gotten lazier. . . ."

Sileki's arms unfolded, and he got to his feet. "I'm doing the best I can with her."

"If the best doesn't win gold medals, then the best isn't the best." He gave his assistant coach a hard stare.

Sileki's eyes grew resentful. "Look, I'm doing everything I can think of to get her to put something into it. But the trouble is that whatever I tell her goes in one ear and out the other. She doesn't want to hear Stanislaw's reports about how fast the East German and Russian kids are coming along in their training. All she knows is that she beats everyone here coming and going. It's gotten so that they all feel they don't stand a chance against her, so why even try? She's the queen bee, and she's got them all spooked. Nobody's making the effort anymore."

Doc Stimpson gazed out the window again. Donna was standing at one side of the pool, not moving. She seemed to be holding back from crossing the deck to where the others were clustered around Crystal, laughing at something.

"You know what? We've got an opportunity staring us right in the face here. Jim, see if you can get a little rivalry going between the new kid on the block and Miss Wonderful. Keep it friendly, but let's see if we can rub the two of them together and make the sparks fly."

"Not a bad idea, Doc. Will do." Jim Sileki looked relieved as he headed out of the office to the inside stairway that led to the pool.

As he descended he saw that Donna was still standing a distance away from the others. She's shy, he thought. Just as he reached the bottom, he saw that Crystal had just noticed her. Crystal hesitated at first, then got up and started to walk over in Donna's direction.

That blonde's got more self-confidence than a freaking movie star, he thought as he watched her stride easily across the deck. Sileki now moved in close enough to observe but not close enough for anybody to pay any attention to him.

"Hi," said Crystal, with a bright, laid-back smile. "I guess you're the newcomer to our ranks. I'm Crystal Delehanty."

Donna was overwhelmed. And grateful for the attention too. "I'm . . . uh . . ."

"Forgot your name?"

Donna tossed back her long brown hair and laughed. "I guess I did for a moment. I'm Donna Wilder. Meeting Crystal Delehanty—whew! That's heavy duty back where I come from."

"Where's that?"

"Nobody's ever heard of it. Not even folks fifteen miles away. Platterkill, a little town in upstate New York. Near Canada."

"They got some good swimmers in Montreal. Ever go there?"

"Once or twice. But not to swim."

"What's your best stroke?" By now other swimmers, mostly girls but one or two of the boys as well, had come up behind her. Only Sabra held back, then she dove into the pool.

"My best stroke?" Donna repeated slowly, feeling as if there were something wrong with her mouth . . . or that maybe she had been struck dumb.

"Yeah. Which one are you strongest at?"

"About the same."

"All of them?" Crystal's eyebrows went up. "Equally good? Or equally bad?"

Donna was getting flustered again. She realized that Crystal was being friendly, but still there was just a *little* edge to her questions. The Golden Girl was sizing her up.

"I dunno. I guess it depends."

"That's being modest. But what's your best time, say, in the fifty-meter freestyle sprint?"

Donna told her.

"Come again?"

Donna told her again.

"What about the . . . two hundred fly?"

Donna told her that, and Crystal blinked. Someone else whistled. Crystal asked Donna her times in a few other events, then broke off. "Well," she said, "I guess you don't need to show up for training at all." She introduced Donna to a few of the other swimmers, then said, "Gotta go," and left the deck to enter the exercise room.

Watching the others walk away, too, Donna felt a little funny about the way their first encounter had gone. But maybe, she told herself, it was just the butterflies in her stomach acting up.

Jim Sileki waited a few minutes. Then he followed the swimmers into the exercise room. Most of them were on the floor mats going through their stretches.

"She's got to be the all-time phony of the world," Crystal was saying. "If anybody's been making times like that—even from that jerkwater place—what's its name? Doesn't matter—I would have heard or read about it."

"Not necessarily," someone said. "The magazines don't pick up everything that goes on. Especially on those—"

"Crystal knows what she's talking about!" Sabra heatedly put in.

Sileki strolled in. "If you people are going to

exercise, exercise. If you're going to yammer, yammer."

"Jim," one of the swimmers called out. "Just one question. What have you heard about Wilder's times?"

"That I don't know about," he said, folding his arms and leaning against a wall. "But I did hear her just say to Doc that Crystal Delehanty is overrated as a swimmer and that she is going to mop up the pool with her in any event they hit together."

The Golden Girl stopped dead in the middle of a bend. "She said what? What did she say?" Crystal bounded to her feet. "I mean, exactly, word for word."

"Word for word," Sileki replied calmly, "I don't remember. But that's what it came down to, more or less."

"Wait a minute." She confronted Sileki at close range, eyeball to eyeball. "Did she or did she not say she was going to mop up the pool with me?"

Sileki thought a moment. "No, I think her exact words were that she'd make you eat all of her waves."

Crystal stood there, dumbfounded. "She actually said that about me?"

He held up his left hand. "Scout's honor."

"It's supposed to be your right hand, Jim," somebody pointed out.

"I'm a lefty, but—" He held up both.

"Crystal," said Sabra, who seemed to be fuming even more than her friend. "Why don't you make her prove it? Put her in her place?"

"You mean, a race?"

"Sure."

"Where is she? Where did she go?"

Sileki shrugged. "Maybe she went over to the dorm. Unpacking, probably."

Crystal made a dash for the lockers, then decided she didn't need to change and hurried out of the building.

Donna had a little trouble finding Evergreen and then locating her room. When she got there, the door was open, her bags were inside, but there was no roommate. She was just deliberating whether to unpack now or fall down dead-tired on the bed when Crystal stormed in behind her.

"Hey, Wilder!" Donna turned. "How about you and me having a little meet of our own? Sort of a welcome-to-the-fold, break-in kind of thing. You know, a little friendly, get-acquainted race, just the two of us. And I'll tell you what. You pick the distance and the stroke. Fair enough?"

Donna looked at her challenger. Crystal was glaring at her, hands on her hips, eyes flashing fire. She couldn't believe this was happening.

"I . . . uh . . . I just got here."

"I know you just got here. That's why I'm letting you pick the distance and the stroke."

"But I'm . . . I haven't practiced for days. And I've been up most of the night on the—"

"Just as I thought!" Crystal cut in with a triumphant sneer. "I knew all along you were a *liar!*"

Donna very rarely lost her temper. But when

she did, she usually became—not hot like most people—but cold as steel. Now her jaws were clenched like two metal sides of a trap. Her voice passed through her tight lips in a low, trembling hiss. "You give me twenty minutes, and I'll meet you at the pool!"

The news of the grudge race spread to all the swimmers—the boys too. From wherever they happened to be they piled into the Mark Spitz Pavilion with grins on their faces. Someone had gotten the Golden Girl mad. Now they wanted to see the pool go up in smoke.

Up above in his office, Doc Stimpson stood watching quietly. Below, Jim Sileki appeared with his starter's pistol. Crystal and Donna stepped up to the blocks—Crystal at lane four, Donna at lane three. Crystal glanced at Donna sharply. "You haven't told me which stroke you want, hotshot."

Donna tossed back her head as she adjusted her bathing cap. "I don't care. You pick it. You're so good at being the boss around here."

"Okay. Your funeral. The two-hundred-meter free."

"You got it." She went into the grab dive crouch.

Sileki held up his pistol. "Swimmers take your marks...." Donna took a quick look at the sidelines and picked a place where she imagined her brother Bret might be sitting, watching, cheering her on. Bret was there. He was there in spirit, she convinced herself. The shot exploded—and she dove.

Donna hadn't swum to win in months. "You're going to take the race, anyway," Bret would always tell her. "Swim against yourself, against your best time." But today she was swimming against another girl. And all she could tell as she surfaced was that Crystal wasn't ahead, wasn't even. Donna was inches ahead. With a surge of energy that was like a feeling of joy, she threw her whole body into her stroke. Her hand hit the water on a slant just perfectly, and as she pulled back, there were no air bubbles at all to slow her down with their drag. Her body was streamlining just the way Bret had taught her. Her kick was in sync. She lifted her opened mouth only high enough, and no more, for her to pull air out of the little depression in the water that her left arm had just made with its pull-back stroke. Everything felt perfect.

And then she sensed that Crystal Delehanty was passing her.

Perhaps she knew from a tremor in the water. She didn't waste a glance to find out how she knew. She didn't need to perk her ears up to hear the shouts of the onlookers. "Let loose! Let loose!" Bret was saying in her head. "It's all in you. Let loose!" Her arms rose and fell like trip-hammers. She went into the flip turn. She knew that in this race she couldn't hold back. She couldn't pace herself. She had to treat this as if it were a sprint all the way. Had to trust that the reserves would be there on the final laps.

Going into the third, she felt for the first

time that she was gaining on Delehanty. By the end of it they were touching the pool's rim together. One lap to go. One lap to beat this vicious, nasty person who had tried to humiliate her for no reason at all.

"Go! Go! Go!" Bret's voice was booming in her ear. "Trust your form. Don't tighten! Loosen up! You can do it!" Suddenly she knew that the girl swimming beside her was turning on a burst of power. Donna was a split second late, the tiniest fraction of a second behind.

"Let loose!"

And she did. Matching Crystal Delehanty stroke for stroke, she overtook the Golden Girl. And at the last instant Donna Wilder stretched out her long arm a hair's whisper ahead of Crystal's thrusting fingertips and took the race.

The swimmers standing by the poolside were stunned. Jim Sileki gazed at the timer clock, then up at Doc Stimpson, still standing at his glass wall. There was a look of satisfaction, nothing more, on the head coach's face as he turned back into his office.

"Great race! Terrific!" said some of the swimmers, a few of whom went over to congratulate the newcomer.

Sileki said nothing to Donna. He had other fish to fry. Walking over to the stunned loser, he cupped his hand to her ear, murmuring, "Doc and I tried to tell you that you didn't have it made, but you wouldn't listen, would you?"

She dodged his hand as if it had been an insect buzzing around her. "Look! She took me by surprise the way she hit the water. I wasn't expecting it and—"

"Hey, no excuses. A loser is a loser. This Donna Wilder came out of nowhere and beat your time. You know what? I think she set this all up to psych you out. I think she's got your number. I think she knows where you live." His thin mustache lifted above his open mouth as he gave her a toothy grin. "Be careful, Golden Girl. She's gunning for your records, the Nationals—and maybe that berth you were so sure of on the Olympic team. She wants it all."

Standing by the pool's edge, Donna Wilder waited. Had Crystal Delehanty taken one step toward her, showed one sign of taking back her nasty remarks, of being gracious, Donna would have met her halfway. She had never in her life gloated over defeating someone in a race. But there was Crystal, sullen-faced, darting angry glances, not at her but at the deck. And there was that other girl, Sabra, looking daggers in her direction as she put her comforting arms around Crystal.

Donna pulled off her cap, tossed back her hair, and called out so loudly that the walls of the pool rang, "Still think I'm a liar, big mouth?"

Chapter Three

Donna had to admit that she savored her victory over the famous Golden Girl. It was the first thing she put in her letter back home to Bret and her parents.

But I haven't been able to make friends with the other swimmers yet. They don't seem to notice that Delehanty is such a sore loser—only that I yelled at her for calling me a liar! Well, I guess that was kind of a dumb thing for me to do. I mean, making it look as if I were gloating. After the race I really was ready to make up with her, only all she did was just stand there.

Donna thought about it a little more, then wrote on.

And that's how it's been ever since classes and practice sessions started up the next day. She went wild when Jim Sileki made me the front swimmer in the freestyle practice. But he was very nice. He just told her in front of everyone that I had made the best time in our race—so I was the lead-off swimmer. It was my job to set the pace—and that was fun!

I'm surprised, Bret, that we're not working much with Doc Stimpson yet. He seems mostly to sit up in his office or go on trips. I guess he wants us to do a lot of practicing before he spends his valuable time with us on our strokes. Although, he does look out of the glass wall a lot, so I guess he's taking notes.

That reminds me about another swimmer. There's this girl, Sabra Siebel. I really feel sorry for her because Doc's put her on probation. She's got to improve if she wants to stay in school. The trouble is, she seems to blame me for her problems, which is really dumb.

Anyway, I think she's a little wacko. She had this beautiful hair, auburn color, really silky. And yesterday she shaved it all off. She thinks she's going to pick up some time in the water by cutting down drag. But so far she hasn't. All it's done is make her look practically bald! So now she has to put a scarf over her head when she goes to class. And a lot of the guys make fun of her in the lunchroom.

I've gone over to her a couple of times when we meet in study hall or on the food line and tried to act friendly. She always just grunts something like, "Excuse me. I have to go now"—and walks off. I guess she thinks Crystal will be mad at her if she talks to me. All the girls on the squad look up to Crystal. The boys too. She's like a leader of a tribe or a cult or something. You know, a guru. It's disgusting.

When I show up someplace where they all are—at the students' building, maybe, or in our own swimmer's lounge—forget it. The kidding around stops. Or they just act as if I'm not even there. Crystal gets louder and louder with her jokes and everybody laughs even more.

It all makes me feel—I don't know—really embarrassed. Oh, well! I'm only going into my second week here.

Anyhow, Maggie, my roommate, is very nice. She's a really good runner. She does a wonderful mile. But she's leaving school today—her mother got very sick, and she has to go home. I really hope that everything will be all right. So now I don't know whether I'll get a new roommate or not. I'd rather have somebody. It gets kind of lonely here.

What else? Oh. Classes are okay. The teachers are all proud of being able to teach here, but I sometimes think they are a little too scared of the kids. Not physically. (Did I spell that right?) I mean, they know that some of us (hey, check me out saying *us!*) are going to be champions someday. And some of them can't deal with that. Makes them walk on eggs—except for the math teacher. He is *strict.*

But the students are pretty good. They don't goof around much. And most of them are really smart. Besides, the dean is always making speeches about how we have to keep up our grades—or else. And so far there's no social life at all—at least not for me. Crystal's having a birthday dinner in town, and I'm the only swimmer who's not invited. But who needs it, right?

So now that I'm at the end of my letter, I guess I ought to tell you the truth. I keep thinking about Gregory. I've left two messages, long distance. I charged it to you, Mom and Dad. Hope you don't mind. But he hasn't called me back. Well, I guess that for him it seems like only a few days since I left. But I feel as if the whole world has changed. It's like a million years.

If you see him, tell him I— No, don't say anything. I'm sure he knows. Anyway, all my love.

Donna

P.S. I miss my stereo. Everyone is blasting their music during homework time at night. And I need mine to drown them out!

She folded the letter into an envelope, addressed it, and walked out of her room. Now where, she asked herself, do you mail things around here? There was no one to ask in the hall. It was deserted. Wonder of wonders, there wasn't even music coming from any of the rooms—a sure sign that everyone was off somewhere. The Student Center must have a mailbox, she thought.

She left Evergreen Hall and stepped into the moonlight. Turning left, she headed across campus toward one of the pyramid-shaped buildings. Her way led past a basketball court, and she stopped for a moment to gaze at a figure weaving in under one of the baskets. He twisted high into the air, and an arm that was almost level with the hoop simply dropped a ball inside. The thin form landed so lightly on the ground that she hardly heard the sneakers making contact. A moment later the huge ball was resting inside some of the longest fingers she had ever seen.

"Hi."

"Hi," she answered as the young man stepped in close enough for her to get a look at him. He was blond, nice-looking, and tall, tall, tall.

"Listen," he said carelessly, "you wanna get married?"

"W-what?" She half laughed, nervously.

"That's just an icebreaker. I saw it in a movie. How about a game?" He held the ball toward her, although a mesh fence stood between them.

"I don't play."

"Well, I figured. It's why I made the offer. That way I can win."

"Thanks, no. I have to go mail a letter."

"It won't go out till Monday, anyway."

She started to walk away. "At least I'll know I sent it."

He tucked the ball under his arm and padded after her. "Mind if I walk with you? I owe so many letters that I want to see what it's like to do my duty. . . . I'm Bo Deaver."

"I'm Donna Wilder."

"I know. I see you in Spanish all the time."

She turned with a puzzled look. "We're in the same class?"

"Sure. You trip over my long legs every day."

"Really?"

"Yeah, it's very bruising. You want to see my kick marks?"

"No, seriously. You're in my class?"

"Must be that mask of invisibility I wear so I won't get called on."

She slapped her head. "No, no—it's me. I guess I'm not really noticing anything these days."

"Who's an any*thing*? I'm an anybody."

"I didn't mean it that way."

"Neither did I."

Donna began to feel like the straight man of a comedy act. She stopped and stared at him. "What's *with* you?"

She was no shrimp, but Bo Deaver towered over her like a tree hanging over a bush. "Me?" He shrugged. "I'm just being difficult. That's why they sent me to this reform school."

Donna's half snort of a laugh quickly changed back to a glum expression. The tall basketball player saw it all. "Having a rough time, Wilder?"

"No . . . well, maybe. Yeah, kind of."

His voice grew gentle as they started to walk again. "Want an arm around your shoulder?"

47

If she was going to let him know about Greg, this was the time. "I have a boyfriend."

"Gee." He fell back for a moment and touched his right palm to his heart. "You sure can devastate a guy pretty fast."

"Just thought I'd get it in." She grinned.

"Guys out here coming on to you all week?"

"No," she admitted.

"Well, what's the matter with them?" he exclaimed.

"Have you got sisters?"

"Three. How did you know?"

"Because you're so smooth. Only boy I know like you has a lot of sisters too."

"They didn't train me in smooth. They trained me in ducking guided missiles."

"Well, anyway," she went on, "you're the first to 'come on' to me—if this is what this is."

He shook his head. "This isn't what it is. This is what is isn't."

"What's that?" she asked dizzily.

"I dunno. What did I just say?"

She took a deep breath. "Do you always tease people like that?"

"Only when I'm trying to kid somebody out of a down mood like you've been in all week."

"You could see that?"

"Ever heard of Moonbeam McCloud?"

"No. I'm sure I shouldn't ask, but who is that?"

"He was a character in an old-time comic strip called *L'il Abner*. There was this little black storm cloud over his head. It followed him wherever he went."

"That's me?"

"It's how I felt my first week or two here—when I saw how much better than me everyone else was."

Donna tossed back her head. "They're not better than me!"

"Hey! How's that for confidence?"

She cocked her head slightly and gazed slantwise at the ground. It was something she always did when she was a little embarrassed. "I . . . I guess you think I'm a bragger."

"No, I think it's great. That's something you have to know—how good you are."

"You didn't hear about my race with Crystal Delehanty?"

"No. I'm not interested in the minor sports."

"Minor?"

He put up his hands in mock defense. "Just kidding."

"Well"—she sighed—"I beat her. And that started a lot of trouble."

"Would it have been better if you had lost?"

"No!"

"There you go!" They had reached the front of the student building, and now he faded back. "See you later."

"I thought you wanted to watch me mail my letter?"

"Well, yes—but I don't think I could handle the thrill of it all. I'll have to do a lot more conditioning first to strengthen my heart." He waggled the fingers of the hand that wasn't holding the basketball, grinned, and jogged away.

What a character! she thought, but she was smiling as she entered the building. After she dropped off her letter Donna followed the sound of music to a packed room where boys and girls were dancing. A boy materialized in front of her—and before long, she had joined the crowd.

It was the same night, and everything was still. Because it was well after curfew time, all the kids, including Donna, were asleep. All, that is, but the two people in the car that was gliding without its lights to a parking space near the dorm. As it came to a stop Crystal dashed out from behind the wheel, hand clapped over her mouth to hold back a laugh that was threatening to explode. Sabra, her roommate, got out on the other side and followed her into the building. She, too, had been wildly laughing in the car—or at least she had been trying to. But now her eyes were wide and anxious.

"Crystal," she said as soon as they were in their room, safe from discovery. "I know you've been awfully busy lately. But I really need some help. Will you show me tomorrow what I'm doing wrong in the water with my elbows? I keep trying to hold them high, but . . ."

Crystal had thrown herself down on her bed, clothes and all. Stuffing a pillow against her mouth, she let out a muffled shriek of laughter. That joke one of the boys had told at the party hadn't seemed so funny at first. But, somehow, when she remembered it now, it was hilarious.

Tears came to her eyes, and her whole body quaked. She was only barely aware that Sabra was standing there going on and on about something....

"Jim Sileki doesn't pay any attention to me anymore. I can't get anyone to really look at my strokes and—"

"Sabra, please!" Crystal rolled over on her back, flinging her arms to her sides. "I don't feel like getting all serious. Not on my birthday, which has maybe two minutes more to go. I'll help you tomorrow, okay? Hey. That was so cool, wasn't it, about the—" And she burst into laughter again.

"You mean," she huffed, "what Al Consella said about my hair and how they could use my head to model billiard balls?"

"No, of course not. Come on—my birthday still has a minute to go. Let up on the swim bit for a change, will you?"

"I'm really sorry I've been such a pain."

"Just promise me one thing," said Crystal, sitting up suddenly. "I'm not going to laugh anymore. But you're not going to *cry*, are you?"

"No, I'm not going to," Sabra said, and burst into tears.

Crystal let her feet drop to the floor. "You know, maybe it was a mistake our rooming together this semester—"

"Don't worry," the other girl said, sobbing. "I'll be out of here soon enough if I can't improve my times!"

Crystal stood up. "Hey, come on. Nobody's going to kick you out of Olympic High. Believe me, you're too important to all of us—you're part of the team. But you've been acting like such a fruitcake lately. You've just got to loosen up. Look, I know! Used to be if *I* tightened up, I'd drag right down to the bottom of the pool. Hey, did you ever see me get an asthmatic attack?"

"No."

"Not *here* you didn't—and you won't—not in *this* school. I don't let anything do that to me anymore. Not even what's-her-face. It was so stupid what you did to your hair, by the way."

"I know."

"Okay, that's over with. It'll grow back. But you can't keep ducking out of classes to go running off to the pool. There's no way I can start doing *your* homework for you when I've got to cram through my own."

"I never asked you to!"

"But you just leave it lying there!"

"Crystal, what am I going to do?"

"You have to start studying more. You have to go to class. And you have to lighten up. What's swimming, anyway? Just a dumb sport."

"That's not all it is to me! And it isn't to you, either."

"Hey, I could walk away from it anytime."

"That isn't true. And you know you haven't been the same person since *she* came to Olympic High."

Crystal gritted her teeth. "I don't want to talk about that. In fact, I don't want to talk about anything right now."

"I'm sorry, Crystal. I'm—"

"Okay."

"Will you help me with my—"

"Yeah. With your strokes, yeah. I said I would, didn't I?" She yanked open the bedside drawer. "Let's not talk anymore, okay? I've got to write a letter."

"Me too." Sabra sniffled.

"Good." Crystal threw herself back down on her stomach, turned on the little pencil flashlight in her left hand, and began to write.

Dear Mom and Dad,

Here is a communication from your wandering child. You know? The one who went to Colorado? Thank you for the check you sent me for my birthday. I would say that I'll treasure it always, except that I spent it. I took the squad and my best friend, Alexandra Hays, the world's greatest gymnast, to dinner with me. We broke our diet in every way possible and had a ball. The waiters brought out a cake with sparklers on it.

I imagine you called today to give me your personal wishes. But I didn't see your message on the notebook on my door.

Anyhow, your Golden Girl has got some competition now, but don't worry, I will be on top again. Crystal Delehanty shall rise again! Like the South after the Civil War, right? Maybe I should add—just to prove that I'm a Californian—for sure, for sure.

Now, if I were going to mail this letter, I probably wouldn't say anything. But since

I am going to crumble it into a little fly speck and toss it in the wastebasket, I will tell you that you two really stink. Scratch that—you're my parents, after all. I will only say that I'm glad I had my birthday without you because at least my friends care about me. Meanwhile look for me in the magazines flashing that toothy grin you bought for me at the orthodontist.

She ended with a flourish, signing it "Crystal el Magnifico"—and crumpled the letter into a little ball.

Sabra didn't see it sail into the basket. Using a bigger flashlight, she was busy writing her letter under the covers.

Dearest Mom,

Please don't worry so much about me and whether I am getting along all right. I'm doing just great! And I'm only sorry that we didn't have more than two weeks to be together when you came out to visit me.

You really got the wrong picture when you came, Mom. Things weren't going too hot for me then. I was just sort of under the weather and not doing my best. But I'm not run down now at all, and my spirits are really up! I've been taking vitamins and getting plenty of rest as I promised you I would.

Guess what? The coach is really pleased with my swimming now! He called me in last week and complimented me on it. There's a new girl who's just come to school—a real natural—and she's been making everyone go fast. It's really been hard on my closest friend in the world, Crystal, who lost her second race to her yesterday, doing the 200-meter butterfly, and she came back to the room crying. But Doc Stimpson says that my speed is picking up better than anyone else's!

I know you think that I'd be better off at home, Mom, but you're wrong. Please be happy for me. I am. Lots and lots and lots of love. All the love a person can have.

Your daughter,
Sabra

Chapter Four

Another week went by, and when Sunday morning rolled around, there was a pounding at Donna's door. "Hey, Wilder! Call for you!"

"Me?" She grunted sleepily. "Who is it?"

"Definitely male!"

Donna threw on a robe and raced out of her room, sure that it was Gregory at last! She snatched up the pay phone receiver dangling from the booth at the other end of the hall. "Hello?"

"Hang in there, kid! Delehanty is just jealous! She's had it too good."

"Bret!"

"Yup! It's me! I thought you'd rather hear my voice than get a letter. Anyway, I sure wanted to hear yours. You got me worried about you."

"I'm . . . all right."

"Uh-huh. What about this rivalry you got going out there?"

"Well, it's pretty heavy."

"Say, you never let a little competition get to you before."

"It isn't that, Bret, it's—"

"I know, I know. It's the bad feelings."
"Yes."
"How did it start?"
"I don't know. She was talking to me nicely and asked me what my best times were. Then a little while later she came over and challenged me and started calling me a liar."

Bret thought a moment. "Well, it does sound a little off the wall. Maybe someone put her up to it."

"What do you mean?"

"Well, what's happening out there? Everybody working harder than they were before?"

"I don't know. I wasn't here before. But maybe. I guess so. Crystal doesn't even practice with the rest of us at afternoon sessions anymore. She does it by herself at night—and I hear that Doc Stimpson is working with her. And I don't think that's fair, either. He's not working with me."

"Who is?"

"A guy named Jim Sileki."

"Sileki? I've heard of him. He knows his business, Donna. The man walked away with a silver medal in the Olympics. And a bronze too."

"But he keeps after me all the time. 'You better watch out, Wilder! Delehanty's got streamlining you can't even touch. Your kicking's out of sync. She'll pass you in a hot flash!' It's driving me nuts!"

"But it's also making you go faster?"

"I guess so. Yes." She lit up for a moment.

"And my butterfly's really improving, Bret. You know how I used to lower my—"

"See what I mean?" he broke in cheerfully.

"Bret, you just don't understand." There was disappointment in her voice.

"Okay, okay—I do understand. It sounds as though the competition's gotten out of hand. I mean, that's not the way to go about it—by making people miserable. Why don't you have a talk with Doc Stimpson?"

"I couldn't do that!"

"Why not?"

"I just couldn't."

"Want me to call him?"

"No, don't! Please."

"Have you thought about speaking to *her?*"

"She hates me!" Donna was getting more frustrated by the second.

"I'm willing to bet that really isn't so. When people respect each other, they usually find it hard to hate at the same time. *And* she must know you're not a liar. All right, so some feelings got hurt. But you're both gonna have to make your peace about that. So go and talk to her."

"You really think I should?"

"What's the worst that could happen?"

"She'd spit in my face or something."

"You could always spit back. And somehow I don't think she will. If she does, you'll only know she wasn't worth talking to."

"Okay . . ."

"Okay, you'll do it?"

"Okay, I'll think about it. How's . . . how is

everybody?" She was thinking about Gregory again.

"The folks are fine. They're off to church. Mom sent you a letter with lots of gossip and hellos from your friends. Also a care package with all kinds of goodies they probably won't even let you eat. And your stereo." He fell silent for a moment, then added, "Yesterday I bumped into your boyfriend."

Donna felt her heart go thump. Was something wrong? "Did he say anything?"

"Nothing much. We're not the world's biggest buddies—"

"Bret!" she cut in anxiously. "You have to give him a chance! He's very nice."

"I'm not saying he's not. I like him. But he doesn't particularly like me."

"Well, he thinks . . ."—her voice dropped to a mumble—"that you pushed me into com—"

"What? I can't hear you."

"Nothing. Just don't be mean to him."

"I'm not—and I wasn't. I just asked him how things are going. And he started muttering, like you just did, and said something about writing you a long letter."

"It hasn't come," she replied in a little voice.

"Well, what can I say?" Bret probably shrugged. "If he's anything like me when it comes to finishing letters . . ." He must have heard Donna's loud sigh, because his tone changed. "Look, kid, you've got your own life to lead out there. I'll bet you've met someone you like already."

"What do you mean?" she asked, reddening slightly.

"What do you mean, what do I mean? A guy."

"No! Absolutely not! I haven't met anyone. And I don't want to!"

"Listen"—he snorted—"when you do *that* much denying..."

Donna gazed quickly down the hall to see if someone might be listening, then whispered into the phone furiously, "Will you stop it? *Yes* I have met someone. But he's only a friend! He knows about Greg. We're strictly friends."

"What can I say?" Bret laughed. "Sounds great to me. Friendship is where it's at. Tell me about him."

"What for? So you can tease me?"

"I won't. I promise."

"His name is Bo Deaver—"

"The basketball player?"

"You heard of him?"

"You kidding? He's team captain out there, isn't he?"

Donna shrugged. "He told me he thought he wasn't a good player."

"What? Why don't you go watch him? Is there a game coming up?"

"Next week. There's a visiting team. But we've got a dual meet at the same time with a swim club that's coming over."

"Listen. Let me know when the biggest meet of the season is. There's got to be a big one, right?"

"I guess so. But why do you—"

"Why?" he shouted. "Because I'm going to fly out and watch you leave them treading water, that's why!"

"You're coming all the way out to Colorado, Bret?"

"Try and stop me!"

"That's ... that's wonderful," she said hoarsely.

"You sure don't sound like it is."

"No ... no, I'm just surprised, that's all."

"I want to watch you climb all over this Golden Girl."

"Oh, Bret, please don't expect that."

"Why not? You're the best, aren't you?"

"Oh, I don't know. Bret, you've never seen anybody swim like her. She goes seven, eight thousand meters, and she never gets tired. She's ... she's like a shark in the water."

"Hey! You already beat her, didn't you?"

"Yes, but she wasn't expecting—"

"Can I believe what I'm hearing? Are you psyching yourself to lose?"

"No!"

"Well, it sure sounds like it. It sounds like you're letting yourself get whipped before you hit the pool. You got to think positive all the time."

"I *am* thinking positive, Bret." But her voice had fallen to a whisper again.

"You know," said her brother, "I don't get upset when you lose to someone else. But I do get upset when you lose to yourself. Champions know better than to let that happen."

"Bret," she lied, "there's someone else here waiting to use the phone. I've got to get off."

"Okay. I love you. Take care. And remember what I said—hang in there."

"I will. I love you too. Kiss Mom and Dad for me."

She hung up and walked away, knowing that she didn't want her brother to come out to watch her compete against Crystal Delehanty. She just didn't need any more pressure.

Donna wasn't alone in feeling pressured. On Monday Sabra received a note from the dean's office, asking her to see Dean Nolan right after classes were over. She could guess already what was coming and just didn't feel she could face it. Although she knew it was a crazy thing to do, she ignored the summons and headed straight for the Mark Spitz building instead. She was just coming out of the locker room in her swimsuit when Sileki called to her.

"Better get dressed again, Sabra. Dean wants to see you right away."

"Can't you tell her to wait until after the session, Jim? I've been working so hard on my breaststroke, and I thought I'd show you—"

But he turned away, shouting to the others. "Okay, warm-ups and stretches! Then check the blackboard!"

As soon as Sileki had mounted the stairs to the office, Sabra jumped into the pool. "What's happening, Sabra?" one of her swim mates asked.

Her laughter sounded a little hysterical. "Who

knows? Probably something stupid, like I used somebody else's food ticket." She swam off.

Five minutes later Doc Stimpson himself appeared at poolside, his bushy eyebrows bristling. He didn't have to blow his whistle for everything to come immediately to a standstill. "Sabra," he said in a voice that was low but firm enough to carry throughout the entire building. "I want you out *now*. And don't you ever disobey an instruction again. Is that clear?"

"Y-yes, sir."

Donna turned to look at the girl treading water there in the pool. All the blood had left her face. It was completely white. As soon as the head coach walked off Donna swam over to her. "Are you okay?" She put a hand on Sabra's shoulder.

"Leave me alone!" Sabra twisted free. "Just stay away from me."

Another swimmer had overheard and now called out, "Hey, Sabra! She was only trying to help."

"I don't need her help!" the wild-eyed girl shouted back as she pulled herself out of the pool and scurried toward the lockers.

With a look of gratitude Donna turned toward Evelyn Tibbit, the teammate who had spoken up for her. This was the first time that any of them had spoken one word of kindness to her. But, as if regretting it, Tibbit immediately dived into the water and surfaced quite a distance away. Now Donna felt even farther apart from the others than before.

For another few minutes or so Donna swam

around, limbering up in the water and trying to put her mind on getting ready for the race that was coming up that weekend. She didn't notice Sabra, dressed now in jeans and a T-shirt, coming out of the lockers and pausing, pale and shaking, on the landing overlooking the pool.

Donna looked up when she heard Sabra screaming her name.

"Wilder! Donna Wilder! You! It's all your fault!" And, covering eyes that were streaming with tears, the girl disappeared back into the office.

After that, it was impossible for Donna to keep her mind on practice. She was too stunned to do more than linger in the pool, treading water and trying to make some sense out of all this. But all that did was put her head in a painful whirl. She had had enough! With a sudden burst of determination she thrust her body out of the water and headed for the steps to the office.

She pushed into the head coach's office without knocking, but this time it wasn't because she had forgotten to be polite. She just couldn't care less.

Stimpson was seated at his desk, finishing a phone conversation, obviously with Dean Nolan.

"Thanks, Margaret," he was saying. "Let's go the extra mile and give her another couple of weeks or so. We'll work together on this."

He hung up the phone. "I guess you can figure out who we were talking about. Is that what you came to ask me about?"

"Yes."

"Look, Donna. Sabra is not your problem—and don't let her turn it into that. I don't know how much of that conversation you heard, but I expect you not to discuss whatever you heard with anyone."

"No, I won't."

"I believe you. You impress me as a straightforward young lady, so I'm trying to be that way with you." He noticed that she wasn't moving from her spot. "Something else?"

"Why is everyone on the squad against me?"

"They're not against you. They're just very protective of Crystal. She can be a pain and all. But they love her."

"Why is *Crystal* against me?" Her eyes were hot. And if it hadn't been for the anger Donna felt, tears would now be gushing out of them.

He gave her a grim smile. "That's something I'm going to have to discuss with Jim. I did ask him to see if he could get a *friendly* rivalry going between you two, but I don't like the way this one is turning out. I'll get back to you, and we'll see what we can do about it."

His eyes locked with hers, and she could tell that he was being totally sincere. She thanked him but still didn't move.

"Well," he said, leaning back. "Let's have it all."

"Why are you working with Crystal and not me?"

"I *will* be working with you—later. But I'll be honest with you." He stood up and looked out over the pool. "Crystal," he said with an almost fatherly gleam in his eye, "is my shining hope for the next Olympics. She can take those Russians and East Germans—and we need her. I've been bringing her along for some time now . . . and I just have to keep working with her."

"Maybe I'd be good enough to make it there, too, if somebody would take the trouble to train me." She couldn't help feeling a bit resentful.

Doc looked at her even harder. "You've got a lot of natural equipment. But my feeling about you from the start has been that you don't know what you really want. Until you do, I'm putting my money on her. That may sound tough, but from my point of view, you're here just to make her work. Now I'm telling it like it is. How you handle that is up to you."

Donna didn't know whether to feel better or worse when she left Coach Stimpson's office. Was he simply playing favorites and using excuses to cover it up? Or was he challenging her? And did she really welcome the challenge? Anyway, she told herself, one good thing had come out of it: He had promised to put a stop to the feud between her and Crystal Delehanty. Or had he? What did he mean by "We'll see what we can do about it?" That sounded sort of fuzzy to her now. Maybe it was all up to her, anyway. And if she didn't keep barging into the coach's office, *nothing* would get done!

She poured out her thoughts later to Bo Deaver; he was always such a good listener. Bo said nothing until they crossed to their favorite corner of the study lounge in the Student Center and sat down with their homework.

"From all I hear, the coach is a pretty great guy. So I'd wait and let him handle it."

Donna nodded and opened her biology book. She put it down a minute later. "Great or not, why do I somehow have the feeling that Doc won't do anything at all?"

"Maybe he won't. But why not wait and find out? Give him some time before you decide he's messing up." He went back to his own book.

"You know what I think?" Donna blurted out.

He looked up patiently. "What?"

"It's very hard to trust people here."

"Thanks a lot."

"I don't mean you," she whispered. "You're simple."

"That's a great compliment."

"No, I mean you don't have a lot of garbage cluttering up your mind. Everyone here has so much happening in their heads, you don't know where they're coming from. Even *I'm* that way!"

"*I* trust you."

"You do?" She smiled.

"Yeah. But not to keep quiet when I'm trying to study."

"If you're not interested, then I'm very sorry." She rose to her feet.

He stared at her. "Do you always get huffy with people you're crazy in love with?"

"I'm not in love with you."

He shook his head. "There's no accounting for taste. Sit down, anyway." She sat, and he put his book aside. "Okay, what were you saying?"

"What I'm thinking is that maybe Bret was right when he said that Crystal was just jealous. But maybe he was wrong too."

"Come again?"

"There might be a lot more to her story than just that. And if we could get to *talk* together . . . and learn about each other . . ."

"Are you working up to going to see her?"

"Yes, and I think I ought to do it before I get too scared again."

"Want to know what I think?"

"Why *else* am I talking to you?"

"Good point," he said, dodging the arrows in her eyes. "What I think is that you were right when you said what you did about all those things going on in people's heads. And Doc Stimpson knows her a lot better than you do. I mean, look—even I've been around her for two years and I don't know her at all. So if I were you, I'd wait—since he said he was going to handle it—and let him handle it."

"You're right," she agreed, slapping her open hand down on the table. "You're absolutely right. I'll wait."

"Fantastico. I am going back to studying now." He opened his book again.

"But I *can't* wait!" She jumped to her feet again.

"That's exactly what I said. Don't wait. Where are you going?"

"To the swimming building."

"May the Force be with you."

* * *

Donna began to lose courage the moment she heard Doc Stimpson's voice booming over the pool. "You're still not doing it, Crystal. That grab start of yours was the problem. If you can't do that right, stick to the regular dive."

"I *can* get it right!" Crystal was insisting.

"Okay. You let Donna get ahead of you that time because when you went forward, you didn't jump *up* high enough. And you didn't arc right. You've got to get those feet up, or you're practically into a jackknife! And then there's no distance at all. Try it again."

Donna stepped silently onto the deck and hung back by the second pool, watching from a distance while Crystal made her dive.

"That's it! Keep going! Go for speed! Go for speed!"

Donna felt her breath catch in her throat. Crystal was streaking across the pool . . . then back . . . then again . . . then back . . . then again. Donna's eyes turned to the sweep hand on the big pace clock. It seemed to be moving in slow motion compared to that shimmering body in the water.

Suddenly Crystal burst up from the pool. "What's *she* doing here?"

The coach turned around. "Donna, I told you that I would—"

"She's spying on me! Get her out!"

"Calm down!" he snapped back at her sternly. "There is something we ought to talk about *now*."

69

"No, nothing! Get her out, or we won't talk about anything. I'll leave the school. I'll go back to California!"

But Doc was not to be bullied. "Don't threaten me, girl. You are still a student here. And if you push me—then you *will be* out." On these last words his voice shook.

Even from a distance Donna clearly saw the shock written on Crystal Delehanty's face. It was as if one of her own parents—or her brother—had suddenly and totally betrayed her. Doc Stimpson was also upset. His hands were clenched; his body had grown rigid. This graying, sixty-year-old man was trying to be fair, but it was costing him a great deal.

"I'm going!" Donna suddenly cried out. "Forget it! I'm going!" She whirled around and rushed away from the pool, leaving the coach and his great shining hope—the Golden Girl—far behind.

Chapter Five

That night Donna had the first of her drowning nightmares. It wasn't a very clear dream. Or rather, she remembered very little of it after she awakened, bathed in sweat. She was in a race where no one seemed to matter except herself and Crystal. And somehow, although she didn't see him, Donna knew that her brother was there, watching.

In the middle of the pool it happened—cramps so terrible that they doubled her over. Then her body grew numb, her arms and legs turned as useless as sticks of wood, and she started to sink beneath the water.

"Bret!" she tried to call out. *"Bret!"* But his name never left her mouth before she went completely under.

He'll come for me. He must! He will!

And suddenly he *was* there! Diving down, down, he wrapped his arms around her and pulled. But she wouldn't move. She was like some boulder that couldn't be lifted off the bottom. Again and again Bret tried, but now his own air was giving out. At last, with a look of terrible despair, he floated up to the surface. And as he deserted her Donna's lungs burst.

Other dreams followed that one. But the feelings of dread the first one had created stayed with her until morning; later they were still half lingering in her mind as she walked to the Student Center to check her mail before going on to class. A letter from Gregory—the one that she'd waited for for so long—was lying in her box, and she tore it open immediately. It wasn't very long.

Dear Donna,
I've taken a lot of time writing this because I really was fighting with myself not to send it at all. But I didn't think that would be fair. It's not that I'm seeing someone else. I haven't had any dates or anything like that. Only, well—I just don't think we should be tied down to each other anymore.

Donna felt her eyes misting over. She had to wipe them before she could read on.

I still care for you. I guess you could say I love you—as much as I ever did. But I suppose I'm a coward. I don't want to wait until I get one of these "Dear John" letters from *you*. My feeling is that you went and I stayed, and that once you started, you'd keep on going. It's just a matter of time. So I want to feel that it's not just something that's happening to me, that I have some control over it. This way it seems more like it's mutual and we're still friends. That part means a lot to me.

Well, I want you to know that I'm really rooting for you, and I'll be looking for your name in the newspapers. Someday I'm going to say, "You guys see that girl on television who won more gold medals than Mark Spitz ever did? We used to go out together!" And I guess that will make me a celebrity too.

Please don't think that I left you at the altar or anything. I don't think little old Platterkill is where you're ever going to end up. Keep stroking, or whatever it is that swimmers say to each other.

Greg

Donna ran straight to her room, fell on her bed, and cried for over an hour. Afterwards she sat up and wrote a letter back to Gregory.

Yes, I am hurt, but I do understand why you feel this way. You thought that at least we'd have the summer together, but we didn't. Greg, darling, that was hard for me too. And you're wrong about where I want to end up. I love Platterkill and I love you! I'm not telling you that you shouldn't see anyone else, but *I'm* not going to. And when I come home for Christmas (I will come home for Christmas!), I'll prove to you that we do belong together. Please, please write to me and tell me what you think.

Your loving Donna

Half of the school day was over by the time she finally showed up at the academic building.

"Do you have an excuse for coming in so late?" the dean asked her when she went to the office for a note.

"No."

"You're not feeling well?"

"I'm fine."

Mrs. Nolan gave her a long look. "Do you remember, Donna, that I asked you to come to me if you had any problems?"

"Yes, I remember."

"Any chance I could be of some help to you now?"

Sure, Donna told her in her thoughts. *Do you know someone who could cut me into two people and send one of me home?* Out loud she said, "I don't think so. But thank you."

"Well, if you should change your mind, just come by anytime." She handed Donna the excuse slip. It simply read, "Permission for late entry. Personal reasons."

Donna paused. "Well, there is something I ... uh ... I would like to ask you."

"Yes?"

"It's about Sabra Siebel."

"Depends on what you want to ask."

"Is she going to be all right?"

"What do you mean, all right?"

"Is there someone who can . . . who can help her with her studies?" But that wasn't Donna's real question. The real one was: Do you think she might do something terrible to herself if they don't let her stay at Olympic High?

The dean looked at her as if she had guessed what Donna actually had in mind. "It's very kind of you to be concerned about Sabra. I can see that it's part of what's weighing you down. I also know something about your problem with Crystal."

She looked at Donna more closely, and her voice grew gentler. "And I very much suspect that you are not far from asking permission to leave school. Is that true?"

The question struck panic into her. For a moment she almost imagined that standing behind the dean were her brother at one shoulder and Gregory at the other.

"You really don't have to answer," said the woman. "But you're not as alone as you think. And if you'd let me, I'd like to be your friend. Go along now."

Bo lifted an eyebrow when she arrived late for Spanish class. As soon as the teacher wasn't looking, he turned a little note into a paper airplane and sailed it over. *"Como esta usted?"* it said. "How are you?"

Donna folded up the note and gave no hint of a reply, not even a shrug. He caught up with her in the hall after class broke up. "What happened with Crystal last night?"

"She blew up at me."

"Figures."

"And Sabra blew up at me before that."

"I know. You told me."

"And now *you're* going to blow up at me."

"Me? No, I'm not. Why should I?"

"Because," she said, looking straight ahead rather than at him, "I can't spend time with you anymore."

"What do you mean?"

"What I said, okay?"

"Did I do something out of line?"

"No."

"Too big a social schedule?"

She turned on him furiously. "Can't you leave me alone?"

He stared at her, then suddenly grinned. "You *are* in love with me."

She felt like hitting him. "Why do you say things like that?"

Bo shrugged. "The only way I can figure out to keep my feelings from being hurt."

"I hurt *everybody's* feelings!" she shouted, and ran off.

"Come on! I didn't mean that!" But she was gone. "I was only kidding," he said to himself aloud, then kicked the wall hard with his sneaker. He turned, his big toe smarting as if it were on fire, and limped away.

Chapter Six

Donna felt terrible about breaking off her friendship with Bo Deaver like that. But what could she do? Bo was obviously interested in her. And hanging out with him made her feel even more hopeless about patching things up with Gregory.

A certain thought was buzzing in her mind—driving her on. If only she could keep herself completely for Greg, then maybe—she didn't know how—by some magic, he would somehow know about it all the way back in Platterkill and would stay away from other girls!

Deep in her heart she knew that this was foolish. But there was just too much happening for her to deal with. Too many confusions about Gregory ... Bo ... Bret ... Sabra ... Crystal! And, most of all, about herself! She didn't want to think anything through right now. And there was no real time, anyway. She needed to practice much harder. The contest with the Warm Springs Club was coming up fast.

The other team wasn't the real problem, though. The meet was expected to be a pushover. But she and Crystal were going to be in some of the same events. And everyone knew that the Golden Girl was out to make Donna look as if she were standing still in the pool.

Maybe Crystal would pull it off too. After all, Doc Stimpson was working with her every night. And Crystal had looked so good in the water! Then, too—although Donna tried to push it out of her mind—there was that ghastly dream.... She couldn't dismiss it from her thoughts. There seemed only one thing to do, and she called her brother on the phone that night.

"Listen, Do-Do," he said in that confident voice of his. "Just forget about it. Every athlete has dreams like that when they get afraid of jamming up. Thing to do is to get off your backside and go ask Sileki to give you some help where you're weakest. You know where those points are. And I'm sure he'll be glad to do it."

Bret was right. The next day the assistant coach practically jumped at the chance of working privately with Donna. Perhaps he was feeling bad about the fact that he had started the rivalry. Perhaps, too, he had a little competition of his own going on ... with Coach Stimpson. If he could help Donna beat out Crystal Delehanty, that would show what *he* could do.

"Let me tell you about being in a race with that lady," he said. "If you stay neck and neck with her, you lose. If you think you're doing fine by pulling a little ahead of her, you lose. I know you came from behind in the last lap in your first race, but you can't count on that with Crystal. You've got to get out in front by a good body length and hold that lead. Because, if you don't, then look out. She'll pass just about anybody in the last lap, as if they were standing still. Crystal's got finishing power you wouldn't believe."

"I believe," Donna said moodily.

"Relax your muscles. I can see that you're tensing up already. Don't get spooked by her like the other swimmers here. Then you've lost from the start."

Donna nodded.

"Be the same cocky kid who walked in here a few weeks ago—and wiped her out because you wouldn't take any garbage. Show that you're not afraid."

Friday night—the night before the meet—she found a note from Bo slipped under her door: "Sorry I can't make it to watch you swim tomorrow, but I've got a suggestion. Forget about Crystal's trying to make you look bad. Only *you* can do that to yourself. Forget about how important it is to win. Because it doesn't mean anything unless *you* say it does. Forget about yourself too! Think only about the water and how good it always feels to do the thing you do as perfectly as you can possibly do it. Also forget about me competing with that boyfriend back in Platterkill. I only want to be your friend. Bo."

How does he know everything that's going on in my head? Donna wondered in astonishment. *How could he have guessed all my feelings?* It was another puzzle, but she heaved a big sigh and went to sleep with the beginning of a smile on her face. Here—thousands of miles away from the only home she had ever known—Donna Wilder had found at least one friend.

She carried the note with her into the locker room the next morning and read it over several times before changing into her swimsuit. Bo's words—like a prayer—brought peace of mind with them, and she tried memorizing them before heading for the mats in the exercise room.

Crystal was there already, doing her stretches. The Golden Girl seemed neither relaxed nor uptight. Just determined. Donna had to resist a nervous desire to bite her lower lip as she, too, began her workout. Every move that Crystal made, even when she simply walked across the floor, seemed powerful.

All at once Crystal stopped to look at her. Donna's heart thumped. *She's trying to psych me out!* she told herself. Then, to stop from becoming frantic, her mind groped for Bo's words. "Forget about Crystal's trying to make you look bad. Only *you* can do that!" Slowly she allowed her eyes to meet Crystal's.

What Donna now saw surprised her. There was no anger in Crystal's stare. No threat. If anything, there was the glimmer of . . . what? Worry? Fear? Well, whatever it was, Crystal didn't allow it to remain there for Donna to make a thing out of. It had vanished, and she was simply studying Donna now. Perhaps trying to size up Donna's own state of mind. And when Crystal turned away to go to the pool for warm-ups, it was with the calm of a champion.

The meet itself began with a big surprise for the overconfident Olympic High team. Several of the visiting Warm Springs swimmers turned out to be excellent. Their team took the first women's race—a relay—without any trouble.

The Olympic High girls and the other students who had come to watch were clearly upset. But Doc Stimpson's face looked positively serene. Neither Crystal nor Donna, his two best girls, had been in that one. The head coach had wanted to give some of his less-gifted swimmers a chance to get into the action. But now, in the 200-meter freestyle, he unleashed these two, plus Evelyn Tibbit, against three of theirs.

"Swimmers, take your marks!" cried the starter, and the gun went off.

It was the Golden Girl—Crystal Delehanty—all the way.

When Donna rose out of the water, she amazed herself by coming out of her loss smiling. The reason didn't puzzle her for long. There was no question that Crystal had swum magnificently. She'd been unbeatable. But Donna, too, had done her very best. Though she hadn't won the race, she *had,* with Bo's advice, won out over some of her worst fears. And no one could say that Crystal had made a fool of her. Donna had come in a close—a very close—second, losing only by the length of a hand. She and Crystal were even now, one and one, in the same swimming event. And maybe that was a good enough opportunity for burying the hatchet. "Congratulations!" she called out, meaning it sincerely.

Several sets of eyes turned to Crystal at once. How would she take it? Her friends knew that she had a big temper. But they also knew she had an even bigger heart....

Crystal wasn't buying Donna's graciousness. She was downright suspicious of it. She stared at Donna's open face and read into it the worst of motives. Wilder was only putting on a public show. Wilder was trying to take the sting out of her loss—trying to remind everybody that the race had been close. And giving the idea that there was more to come, that she hadn't been knocked out of the box yet!

Crystal nodded back coldly, before she turned away to her other well-wishers. All right, there had been a win just now but no real triumph. Well, hang on, folks, there soon will be!

True to the promise she had made herself, Crystal took the next race they were in together as well. And this time she left the second-place Donna trailing even farther behind.

Crystal turned her gaze Donna's way. Well, Big Mouth wasn't calling out any congratulations *now*, she told herself. So much for honesty.

Still, something troubled her. Was it the pain and bewilderment she saw in Donna's eyes? Certainly it had something to do with the explanation Doc Stimpson had tried to give her about how he and Sileki had been the ones responsible for the feud. So why was she still keeping it going? Because she didn't *like* Donna

Wilder, that's why! Because Wilder had sneered at her in front of everyone after that first race! Because of the way she had been so sneaky and spied on her the other night. And because ... well, she didn't know why, exactly. But that was just the way it was!

Donna Wilder was never going to take Crystal Delehanty's place in the sun. Never!

Crystal carried her stoked-up anger with her into the next race. Perhaps the fact that she was dwelling on it so did something to her timing. Or perhaps it was just something that exploded inside Donna as the starter's gun went off. But from the moment they hit the water, Crystal sensed without seeing that Donna Wilder was way out ahead of her. *That's all right,* Crystal told herself. *I'll get her. I'll get her!*

But she didn't. At the last lap she was still half a body length behind. Of course, Jim Sileki had been right. That had never been enough to save anyone from her powerful stroke once she opened up. Now Crystal did. But so did Donna Wilder—with a final surge of her own! When Crystal came up out of the pool, it was to learn that Donna Wilder had taken the race.

But Crystal vowed that she wasn't through. There were other events to go—not all of which they were in together. When the meet was finally over, Crystal knew she would be able to say to herself that she had won more races than Donna. But there was one thing she couldn't deny. Now there were clearly two swimming stars at Olympic High.

Standing apart from the others, Crystal tried

to sort out her feelings. How much of this was really being piggy—trying to hog all of the limelight for herself? She'd always resented that sort of selfishness in others. She'd always been the first to go up and congratulate someone who'd done anything well. So why not now?

She had no answer for it. And, as she had done at so many other meets, she now found herself looking around the bleachers. Maybe this time—by some miracle—her father and mother would be there. They hadn't shown up for her birthday naturally, although *this* time she'd had a premonition they would. But couldn't there be a surprise now?—a surprise for the daughter everyone under the sun had been telling them was so wonderful, so beautiful, so . . . She sprang out of the pool.

Crystal noticed her best friend in the world, Alexandra Hays, coming toward her. The grin that shone all over that bright-eyed baby face of hers simply lit it up. Now Crystal smiled too. Alex was perhaps the best athlete in all Olympic High—an almost surefire future gold medalist in every gymnastic event she would enter. Alex's approval meant everything to her. It was almost like having her parents—

Suddenly Crystal gasped. Alex was congratulating Donna. Hugging her! Crystal turned abruptly and headed for the showers.

Alex came bouncing right after her. "Hey, wait up! Wait!" Overtaking Crystal on the run, she tried embracing her from behind, but the Golden Girl shook her off.

"You're a traitor!" Crystal cried. "And I don't need hugs from traitors!"

Alex fell away. "Are you crazy? Have you got some chlorine in your brain? What are you screaming about?"

"I'm not screaming," Crystal rasped, whirling around. "You went over to *her* before you even came over to me!"

"Who's *her?*"

"You know who! *Donna Wilder!*" Crystal shouted so loudly that people all around them turned to look.

"So? She was the first one I passed."

"You told her she was fabulous, too, right?"

Her friend saw that Crystal's jaw was trembling. "Hey, take it easy," she said slowly. "All I said to her was that I thought she had terrific form. That she moved very gracefully. All of which was true ... and I don't see what that takes away from you and why I shouldn't say it."

"Because you are supposed to be *my* friend!"

"What's that got to do with telling another athlete that you appreciate what she's accomplished? We all need that kind of support, don't we?"

"What I need ... what I need," Crystal sputtered, "is for my friends to be loyal!"

"Crystal, what's the matter with you? You were never this way before."

"Maybe I didn't need to have a real friend before."

"You walked away with most of the wins."

"You don't understand! You just don't understand!"

"No, I don't. I'm your friend. But I'm not a lapdog. If I see someone who does something I like, I'm going to tell her. And you're going to have to handle that."

"I do *not* have to handle that! And I don't have to handle you!"

"Really?"

Crystal looked around. She realized now that people were staring at her. Worst of all, Donna Wilder was staring. "Really!" She turned and ran from the pool.

Chapter Seven

The food line at the cafeteria was getting longer by the second. But the Golden Girl still didn't get up from her usual seat at the swimmers' favorite table.

"What's with her?" Ellen Navone, the team's best distance swimmer, whispered to another girl. The two of them were already eating.

Her companion gave a nod toward the checkout counter. Alex Hays was standing there handing her food ticket to the woman who punched them.

"I think Crystal's waiting to see if Alex comes over to apologize."

But the tiny gymnast stepped from the front of the line with her tray and crossed directly past their table without so much as a glance at her former best friend. The girls glanced at Crystal. Her jaw was tightly set, and although she had kept her head facing in the same direction, they could see her eyeballs swiveling.

The next one off the line was Sabra Siebel, her head wrapped up in the scarf she always wore now. She seemed in a big hurry, and as soon as her ticket was punched, she came rushing over to Crystal. "I got this for you," she said, handing over everything on her tray but a glass of orange juice and a slice of buttered toast.

"Thanks," Crystal murmured absently, her gaze still trailing Alex Hays's movements.

Still standing there, Sabra ripped the aluminum-foil covering off the juice. "Aren't you going to sit down and eat?" one of the other swimmers asked. But Sabra gulped down her juice, shifting nervously from foot to foot.

"No. I don't like to swim on a full stomach."

Ellen Navone looked up. "You're going swimming *now?*"

"That's right." Sabra, still standing up, had stuffed the piece of toast in her mouth, and now she chewed as she spoke. "They can't suspend me for skipping *lunch,* can they?"

"But you've only got forty-five minutes."

Sabra glanced up at the wall clock. "Forty now." She took a huge swallow, which must have stuck halfway down because the words came out in a croak. "Gotta go."

"Wait a minute," said Crystal, rising. "I'll go with you and help you with the butterfly."

Sabra lit up. "Oh, would you!" Gratitude leapt from her wide hazel eyes.

"What about your meal?" the person sitting next to her tray asked.

Crystal shoved it over. "Not hungry."

"My God!" Ellen Navone joked. "If Delehanty doesn't want to eat, it must be the end of the world!"

Crystal shot her a withering look, then started off with Sabra. But they hadn't taken more than two or three steps before Crystal stopped short and stared. Alex Hays hadn't settled on a place to sit yet. She'd been weaving through the large cafeteria, greeting people. But now she came to a halt in front of a little side table where Bo Deaver and Donna were sitting off by themselves. The bouncy gymnast seemed in no hurry to move on again. She lingered there, chatting away with Donna.

"They look real buddy-buddy these days," Crystal muttered under her breath.

Sabra was impatient to hurry on, but what could she do? "You mean Bo Deaver and Wilder?"

"No," Crystal hissed, "that's not what I mean."

"Oh, forget about her!" Sabra exclaimed. "I never thought she was a nice person, anyway. And she proved it by the way she treated you at the meet."

Crystal turned to her for a moment. There was doubt in her eyes. "Then you don't think I made too much of it? I mean, you do think she *was* being hypocritical?"

"Well, it was hurtful!" Sabra answered heatedly. "I felt hurt for you—just the way you must have felt hurt for me when I was the only one Doc and Jim wouldn't let swim at the meet!"

If she was expecting Crystal to say something in agreement, it didn't happen. Crystal had gone back to watching the three people at that table. "Come on, Crystal, let's go," Sabra prodded.

"No, wait a minute. I want to see if they're talking about me."

"Who cares about them!" Sabra blurted out anxiously. She took Crystal by the arm and tried to lead her away. "You can't even tell from here, anyway."

But Crystal wouldn't budge. "Oh, I can tell, believe me."

Her voice had turned grim as she watched Alex bursting into laughter at something Bo Deaver said. Bo was laughing, and Donna had a soft smile on her face. Now Alex was getting ready to leave them. But first she rested her tray on the table and did something that sent a pang right through Crystal's heart. She gave Donna a warm, reassuring squeeze on the shoulder and leaned over to kiss her cheek! Then off she went. But Crystal lingered on. She seemed rooted to the spot. "Come on," Sabra pleaded. "I don't have much time."

"I'm sorry. But can we do this a little later? I'm just not into it right now." Her voice was ragged.

"But you said—"

"I'll meet you after my session with Doc, all right? I will, I will—I really promise."

"Every time you say that, there's always something else—"

"I know, I know. Things keep coming up. But tonight I'll really—"

"Oh, yeah. Sure. *Sure* you will!" cried the unhappy girl, stepping backward.

"Look, I said I will."

"It's getting later and later!" Sabra whirled around and dashed out of the building.

Crystal stood there in the middle of the aisle, realizing that she was definitely not handling things well. Something was happening to her. Where had all her calmness gone? All that easygoing charm people were always complimenting her on? Not even her terrific showing at the swim meet had brought it all back to her. Something comfortable, something secure about her life here at Olympic High was vanishing, and she didn't like it at all. She hated it!

"Those two are an item for the *Gazette*," a familiar voice buzzed in her ear.

Crystal turned around. It was Norma Trafficante, the volleyballer who doubled as school reporter. Norma was obviously talking about Donna and the basketball player. It shifted Crystal's attention.

"How long has it been going on, Norma?"

"Not long. But hot and heavy."

But Crystal knew enough to be wary. Norma had a habit of sounding very certain of her facts, even when she was dead wrong. "How can you tell?"

"Look at them."

Crystal was doing just that. The pair were sitting close, very close. In fact, there were only a few inches between their lips. And now Donna, on a sudden impulse, was reaching out to take both of Bo's enormous hands in hers.

"Interesting," mumbled Crystal, setting her jaw. "Very, very interesting."

* * *

The conversation going on between Donna and Bo Deaver was not exactly what it looked like from thirty or so feet away. "What's the matter?" Bo had asked her a moment or two after Alex had walked away.

"Nothing." But her tone was sad.

"That's some kind of a heavy-duty nothing, Moonbeam, old girl."

Donna pushed the food on her plate around with her fork, and she sighed. "Oh, I don't know."

"Neither do I until you tell me."

"Well ... it's ..." She paused a moment, then started again. "It's very nice to have somebody like Alex come over and tell me how well I'm doing and how great I am. And ... that does make me feel good. ... And so does winning."

"But?"

"But it's like what you were talking about in your letter. A person should be feeling good about just *doing* it. And I don't know that I even like swimming anymore. I just don't know."

"Yeah, but show me somebody who adores nonstop practicing every day and I'll show you a certifiable fruitcake."

Donna managed to return his grin with a little one of her own. "But it's not just the practicing, Bo. It's ... oh, I don't know. I give up. ..." Her voice trailed off. Bo looked as if he had something to say, but he was obviously holding back. "What is it?" she finally asked.

"Well, it's kinda really none of my business."

"No, tell me." She leaned closer to him.

"Well, you said the other day that I was a classy advice giver . . ."

"You are!" It was at this point when Crystal saw Donna impulsively grab Bo's hands and squeeze them. "You really are. You don't know how much you helped me at the meet. I mean, your advice was wonderful."

"Want some more?"

"Of course I do!"

"Look. You're *here* . . . and Gregory is *there*. Let it slide."

"I don't know that I really want to hear this," she snapped.

He took a deep breath. "Okay. You're here and your brother is there. Let *that* slide. For a while, I mean. Forget about how proud you want to make him of you."

"I know you mean well," said Donna, looking this way and that, very nervously.

"Forget I said anything. Let's just eat our lunch." But she got to her feet. "Where are you going, Donna?"

"Me?" she said in a dazed voice. "Nowhere."

"So why are you standing up?"

"Oh . . . I just want to go outside and get a little air before class starts again."

"Good idea." He began to get up too.

"No . . . I . . . well, I just want to be by myself for a little while. Is that all right?"

Bo shrugged.

"You're not mad?"

"Who, me? Will I see you later tonight at the

study room? Our usual heavy date? I'll bring the books and you bring the pens?"

She hesitated. "I ... uh ... I think my mom is going to give me a call. So I want to wait around for it."

"Meet you at your room, then?"

"My room?"

"If we leave the door open, nobody will hassle us. But we can ask first."

"No, Bo, I ..."

"Right. You'd rather be alone when 'Mom' calls."

"All right—if Gregory calls. You *are* mad at me."

He stretched out his long legs and studied his distant feet. "You know, it's so hard being absolutely stunningly perfect most of the time that I don't always make it...."

"Bo, I really want to be your friend. But, if I'm hurting you, are you *sure* we should be spending all this time together?"

"Yeah, I'm sure. Only it may turn out to be harder on you than on me."

"Why do you say that?"

"Well, if we're only just 'friends,' like you say, then I'm free to go out with whoever I want to, right?"

"Yes, I guess so...." Her voice trailed off.

He was staring at her. "You don't look any too happy about that idea at all."

"I ... I didn't say that."

"So what do you say?"

"It's not up to me."

"I think what it amounts to is that you don't

want to be with me that way, but then you don't want me to be with anybody else, either. Am I wrong?"

"Do I sound rotten?" she asked in a little voice.

He gave a little snorting laugh.

"No, but it's ridiculous!"

"I know," she said as she started to leave. "I know—and I'm sorry. I know I'm being frustrating!"

Bo gave a sad smile of agreement as he watched her go. Then he reached for the food that she had left on her plate and added it to the pile on his own. "Women!"

Ellen Navone was standing by the front door just as Bo came out of the school building. They weren't close friends, but she knew him well enough. They'd gone to school together in Pittsburgh.

"Hey, handsome!" she called, stepping forward. "I've got a problem for a real macho man to solve."

Bo turned around and looked behind him.

"No, it's *you* I'm talking to. I remember you used to work in your father's garage."

"No, in his print shop."

"Same difference. Come with me."

"Printing problem?"

"No, car problem."

"Listen," he said, stopping. "I don't know anything about cars. And I've got to get to practice."

"Just take a minute! Come on. Don't be a poop."

"Okay. A minute, that's it. Where's this vehicle of yours?"

"Not mine," she said, pointing at the gorgeous back of a girl who was leaning over the engine of a Toyota. "Crystal," she sang out. "Maybe Bo can help."

The Golden Girl looked up, brushed back the strands of straw-colored hair that had fallen over her sky-blue eyes, and gave him a very convincing helpless look. "Oh, would you please? I've been working on this for the past five minutes, and I keep thinking I'm making it worse. Can you believe a car that won't start in the middle of summer?"

Bo slowed his steps, looked at her, then stepped past her. "You check to see if there's enough water in the cells?"

"No. Are you supposed to do that?"

He lifted the plastic caps off one by one. The water level was just fine. Then he inspected the metal ends of the cables that carried the spark from the battery to the engine. "This one is too loose," he said at last. "Have you got some pliers or a monkey wrench I can tighten it with?"

She shook her head, then stepped in close to him—very close—as she, too, gazed down at the terminal. "No, I'm afraid not," she said in a worried tone. "Does that mean you can't fix it?"

A faint scent of flowers seemed to rise from her body. He bent more closely over the battery. "No, I think I can just wedge it on. There. Why don't you try it now and see if it starts?"

As he straightened up he noticed for the first time that Ellen was no longer standing there with them. She was already quite a distance away, jogging off toward the swimming building.

Suddenly the engine roared into action—and the famous smile that had at one time or another dazzled every male within ten miles of Olympic High flashed across Crystal's face. "Yay, team! Bo, that was really nice of you. Thank you so much."

"No problem." He slammed down the hood and started to turn away.

She leaned her head out the window. "Listen, Bo, you headed for practice?"

"Where else?"

"Hop in, I'll drive you over."

"That's okay. I can use the exercise."

"No, come on. I'm the one who made you late." She pushed open the passenger-side door.

"Okay." He jammed himself in, and his knees rose to the level of the dashboard. "They sure didn't build these cars with me in mind."

"Oh, you must be so uncomfortable. Look, pull that lever below your seat. It'll slide back. Never mind, you're too stuck. I'll do it."

She leaned over him again, so close, showing him the long, lovely nape of her neck.

"You know," she said, straightening up to let her eyes momentarily make contact with his, "we've been in this place together for two years and never really gotten to know each other at all."

"Well, we travel in different circles. I'm in hoops and you're in pools."

"I like that. You have a wonderful sense of humor."

"Fear makes me funny."

"Fear of what?"

"Of beautiful girls who come on to me."

Crystal darted him a quick look, then started driving. "You think I'm coming on to you?"

"Yeah. Aren't you?"

"Maybe. I've thought of you a bunch of times when Ellen's talked about you. And I've watched you play, too, did you know that?"

"Yep. I know when you're around."

"I hope that's a compliment."

Bo took a deep breath. "Oh, yes."

She let her hand momentarily rest on his. "How come you never approached me?"

Bo shrugged.

"Are you shy?"

"In some ways, I guess."

"Not on the court, though. You take it over. You're really marvelous."

"I'm just higher than the basket," he said, but a grin was spreading on his face.

"Are you really this modest, Bo? Or is it an act?"

"It's an act. Hides my big ego."

"Well *that's* honest!" She laughed. "Now I know why you didn't ever speak to me. You just think all women should come to you!" She patted his hand again. "But that's all right. I feel very confident myself. Besides, I think you're very nice." She glanced at him. "I mean, worth the trouble."

"Who, me? I'm no trouble."

She laughed again, but then her eyes suddenly opened wide—and she pointed at one of the mountain peaks that soared behind the sports complex. "Oh, look!" she said in a tone that was filled with wonder.

"What is it?"

"Up there on that slope. That cluster of pinks and pale blues. There must be thousands of wild flowers. Do you ever hike that trail?"

"I love to hike. But I don't get much chance here."

She beamed her glittering smile into the rearview mirror, and it showered down on him. "Want to take a hike with me after practice?"

Bo's head swung to the right. Huge, dark clouds were beginning to roll up over the mountains from the south. Soon they would blot out the clear Colorado sky. "I think we're in for some thunderstorms."

"It'll clear up by five or so. Always does."

"Well"—he hesitated—"I've got this exam to prepare for."

She grew silent, then said in a hurt tone, "Would you rather I hadn't asked?"

"Oh, no. It's not that. Really! But I've got to study. I'm having a bad time with physics."

"My dad's a physicist."

"Yeah?"

"I grew up on that stuff. Why don't we meet after practice and I'll go over it with you?"

"Sure! Student lounge?"

"No, somewhere where we can be comfortable. I know. It's very quiet down at Wishing Rock. You know, by the waterfall...."

"It might be a little dark to see what we're doing by then."

Crystal's head turned sideways—just a little. "Who knows," she said with a smile. "Maybe the moon will be out."

Chapter Eight

Mrs. Nolan showed up at one of Sabra's classes a few days later and personally escorted her back to her office. "Sabra," she said as soon as the door was shut behind them, "I'm not going to mince words with you. We gave you another chance to improve in your studies, and you were warned what would happen if you cut any more classes."

"Mrs. Nolan, wait—"

"I don't want to wait, Sabra."

"All I did was come back late from lunch."

"You were an *hour* late."

"I lost track of the time."

"You went to the pool. That was against the rules."

"Even during *lunch?*"

"If you had extra time, you could have used it to study. But, all right, let's say that that wasn't made clear to you. You also had two other cuts this week."

"No, Mrs. Nolan. That's not true. I was having my allergy attacks. And I asked for permission to go back to my dorm and get some medicine and lie down. I had slips from the nurse both times."

"Sabra, you didn't go back to the dorm, you went to the pool area. We checked on you."

"That's not fair! You shouldn't have done that!"

"Our actions aren't really what we're discussing here, are they, Sabra?"

"Maybe they should be! Why are you picking on *me*?"

"Do you think, Sabra, that you can really get the most out of Olympic High with that sort of attitude?"

Sabra turned ash white. "You're not . . . not going to expel me, are you?"

"No." Mrs. Nolan sighed. "Not that, but we are going to have to suspend you from all—*all* athletic activities, Sabra."

Sabra's voice dropped to a croak. "That's the same thing."

"No, it isn't. Or, at least, that's up to you. You can return to swimming after you've made up all your back assignments and taken over the quizzes you've failed and passed them. You'll also have to prove to us for a few weeks that you're keeping up with your current work and doing well at it. Each teacher will have to send me a letter confirming that."

Sabra was desperate. "Mrs. Nolan, you don't understand. If I have to do all that, I'll miss so much practice that Doc Stimpson will drop me from the squad. Then I'll be out of school, anyway!"

"I hope that doesn't happen, Sabra. But there's

nothing I can do about it. We'll have to take it step by step and see."

"Oh, please, don't drop me from athletics!"

"I'm sorry, Sabra, but—"

Suddenly the girl flared. "If I were a terrific swimmer like Crystal and Donna Wilder, would you be doing this?"

Mrs. Nolan glanced sharply at her but only for a moment—and her voice was controlled when she spoke. "I certainly would. Obviously athletics are important at Olympic High, but that doesn't mean we would ease the academic requirements for anyone, even the superstars."

Mrs. Nolan fell silent for a moment, then began again. "I really am saddened by what you've been going through, Sabra. But I think you have to ask yourself if it's necessary. Not everyone is helped by being here at Olympic High. Some are hurt. That is, they're hurt if they stay on when it isn't right for them."

"Please, I don't want to hear—"

"I'm sorry, but I think you should hear what I have to say. A person is going to be happiest if she is where she can function the best. And if you lie to yourself about that—about what your real capacities are—then you will do terrible harm to yourself. Dreams are not enough, Sabra."

"I got into this school, didn't I?"

"Yes, you did. But perhaps that was our mistake."

She picked up Sabra's record, which was lying on the desk. "In junior high school you were an A student. Your test scores were very high.

Your aptitude in computers and science were excellent. Your IQ scores put you among our brightest students. And you had no behavioral problems in your other school."

"I'm not a behavior problem, Mrs. Nolan. Really I'm not. I—"

Mrs. Nolan's voice grew gentle. "You've done some questionable things here, Sabra. Shaving your head, for example. That was an extreme thing to do. And you've refused to see the school psychologist every time I've tried to set up an appointment for you. I think the time has come for us to get in touch with your mother so that we can start thinking about—"

Sabra jumped to her feet. "You can't do that! My mother's a sick woman! You don't know what that will do to her!"

"Your mother is very interested in what is going on, Sabra. She told me that when she visited here, and—"

"She's had crack-ups! My mother has had crack-ups! I don't want her to get upset!"

"I think she'd want to be informed about—"

"Mrs. Nolan, if you write to my mother, I'll ... I'll—"

"You'll do what, Sabra?"

"Just please don't write to her, that's all."

The dean studied the girl's anxious face. "All right," she said at last, "I won't, for now."

"Can ... can I go back to my class, please?"

"Yes, you *may*. Please don't think of this suspension as a punishment, Sabra. It's really for your own good."

Sabra paused at the door and stared at her

with those wide, popping eyes. "I know you think so, Mrs. Nolan. But you're wrong."

For the rest of the school day Sabra felt as though she were in a fog. And afterward, when there was all the time in the world to study, the words on the pages just didn't make any sense. Wandering the campus instead, Sabra watched everyone else at afternoon practice. At dinnertime her heart felt so heavy, she couldn't bring herself to sit among all the happy kids in the cafeteria. She cut the meal altogether and stayed by herself in her room until it got quite late.

It was an hour before bedtime when she heard laughter in the hall. The door opened, and Crystal entered with Ellen Navone and Barbara, another swimmer.

"Hi, Sabra," they said, more or less together.

"Hi."

Ellen plunked herself down on Crystal's bed and continued the conversation that had been going on. "Those divers are such show-offs! And snobs too!"

"Probably," chimed in the other girl, "it's because they stand on those high diving boards all the time. They get used to looking down on us."

"Yes, they think we're so-oo lower class."

"Except when one of the boys wants to go out with us," Barbara tittered. "And they're *all* in love with Crystal. Right, Crystal?"

"If you say so."

"But she puts them in their place," said Ellen. "Crystal, do you ever go out with divers?"

"Not if I can help it!" Crystal laughed. "Did you ever date a diver, Sabra?"

"No," came the sulky answer.

"What's with you?"

"Nothing. Everything's terrific."

But Sabra's back remained turned to them. The other girls looked at one another and shrugged. Ellen Navone propped herself up on one arm and a pillow. "So, Crystal, what's the latest on your secret romance with Big Bo Deaver?"

"That's it. It's a *secret*."

"Not from *us,* it isn't." Barbara snickered. "From Donna Wilder, maybe."

"From her *definitely*," Ellen piped. "That's the whole idea. Crystal, you sure you don't really want him? He's awful cute."

The Golden Girl's face grew serious. "If he cheats on his own girlfriend, maybe he'd do the same to me. I like people to be loyal."

"But not vice versa," Sabra grumbled to herself very softly.

"What?" Crystal asked. "What did you say, Sabra?"

"Nothing."

"But *you* got him away from her," Ellen went on. "Now he's eating out of your hand—and you don't want him?"

"I didn't say that. I'll have to think about it. First things first."

"Like what?"

Crystal gazed at them meaningfully. "Doc is tossing his annual dinner on Saturday just before the end-of-summer dance."

"So?"

A slow grin began to spread across Crystal's face. "So everyone from the team will be there, including Ms. Donna Wilder."

Suddenly Ellen caught on. "Bo's coming!"

Crystal beamed.

"He's picking you up to take you to the dance!"

"You got it."

"In front of *her?*"

A look of triumph flashed in Crystal's eyes. "You'd better believe it."

"But I thought that this love affair was a secret?" said Barbara.

"That's when it jumps right out of the box. Pop! Quite a surprise for Donna, huh?"

"She'll absolutely freak," exclaimed Ellen. "Such humiliation!"

Crystal's eyes glittered. "Couldn't happen to a nicer person."

But Barbara was troubled. "You sure you want to go through with something like that?"

"You think it's cruel?"

"Well, yeah. I guess so. Kind of."

"So was taking my friend Alex away from me in front of everyone!"

"Maybe," Ellen ventured softly. "But that was more Alex's fault than hers."

Crystal glared at them. "Didn't you see how Wilder gloated over it?"

"No, I . . . I wasn't facing her," Ellen mumbled.

"Me, either. She had her back to me."

Crystal's hard gaze didn't soften. "You people with me or not? Are you my friends or aren't you?"

"Sure we are."

"Well, sure, Crystal. We only—"

"Sabra, what about you?"

Sabra had kept her back to them all the while. She didn't turn. "What about me? *What?*"

"Didn't you hear what we were talking about?"

"Do you ever hear what *I'm* talking about, Crystal?"

A heavy silence fell over the room. Crystal took a deep breath. "Are you getting dramatic again, Sabra?"

"Me? No. What have I got to get dramatic about?"

"You've been making remarks under your breath ever since we got here."

Sabra whirled around. "I've been suspended!"

"*What?*"

"You know what that means, don't you?" She was rapidly growing hysterical. "You know how long I'll last now!"

Ellen sat up quickly. "I'm really sorry."

"So am I," Barbara echoed.

But Sabra couldn't care less about them. Her eyes locked upon Crystal. "Over and over you promised to help me, and you never did. You promised me in the cafeteria that you were going to show up at the pool that night. And I waited. And you didn't even come!"

"Sabra, I forgot—"

"You didn't forget. You didn't care! All you could think about was your scheme to get even with Donna Wilder!"

"Isn't . . . isn't there anything I can do now?"

"Like what? I'm barred from the pool. You can't help me there."

"Yes, I can. I'll speak to the dean. She always acts friendly to me."

"Will you please stop pretending? You just say you'd speak to her. You never would. And it wouldn't do any good, anyway. I've got to make up all my homework . . . and catch up on everything . . . and take my tests over. I can't even think straight. There's no way I can get through any of it."

"Yes, you will! Show me what you have to hand in tomorrow. I'll work with you on it—and all the back stuff too."

"So will I," chimed in Ellen.

"Me too," added Barbara.

"We'll divide it up and write it out. Then you can recopy it after we explain it to you."

"Why don't we get some other girls to help too?" suggested Barbara. "Each one can pick the subject she's best in to tutor Sabra on."

"Right!" Crystal was excited now. This was the kind of challenge she could throw herself into. "And that boring stuff that puts you to sleep when you try to plow through it—you know, the chapters you've skipped and all? We'll do that out loud and keep each other awake. And listen, don't sweat the pool. We can drag the dry swimming machine up here, and I'll run you through the strokes right here in the room!"

With a cry of joy Sabra flew into Crystal's arms. The other girls came up to surround them, and soon they all had their arms around one another, embracing.

Chapter Nine

The special dinner Doc Stimpson threw for his team was held in the same elegant restaurant where Crystal had had her birthday party. The table stretched off into the distance, and every one of the forty or so people gathered around it suspected that this was also Doc's birthday—or at least the week of it.

"Not true," insisted the head coach when, toward the end of supper, a few kids tried to tease him into admitting that he was a "birthday boy."

"The reason why I always hold this wingding along about now is that it's still close to the start of our school year, but it's also far enough along to get an idea of the kind of problems we're going to be having."

He paused for a moment and gazed down the length of the table at all the young men and women he and his two assistant coaches were helping to train. "This is a good time to think about these things because the big meet with that San Diego crowd is going to be coming up soon. You know," he said, grinning, "that deluded bunch who think that they are still the prime pipeline of American swimming talent to the Olympics. And what does a *mere* high school team think it's doing by trying to horn in on *their* act?"

Everyone burst out laughing.

"I'm talking, of course, about that slimy group that is trying to steal *you*, Billy Sanders, and *you*, our little Golden Girl, away from us. Never happen—will it, people?"

"No!" came a chorus of voices.

"And, you know"—he chuckled—"I've got a pretty good notion that soon they'll be talking, maybe, to a certain upstart from upstate New York too. So I guess we're doing something right!"

There was more laughter.

"Incidentally, Donna, your brother gave me a call, and he's going to be flying out to catch the meet. Did you know that?"

"No, I didn't," murmured Donna, the smile fading from her face.

"Don't let it throw you," whispered Jim Sileki, who was sitting next to her. He was being extra sweet these days. "Do you want me to find a nice way to ask him not to come?"

"I . . . uh . . ."

"We'll talk about it later."

"Anyway," Doc went on, "I know that *they* can't break us up. But what I'm not so sure of is if *we* can break us up. I mean, is it possible that we could destroy our own team spirit?"

His speech had turned very serious now, and all murmuring stopped. All the kids at the table were pretty sure they knew what he was talking about: Crystal and Donna.

"It's very important," he went on, "to keep a sense of ourselves as a group ... a unit in which all of us care about the next guy even if, in races, we compete against one another. And listen, boys and girls—that is exactly what is expected of all Americans who represent their country at the Olympics. Sure, in each event the players race against one another for their individual medals. And they race against the records other Americans may have already set—sometimes even against their own past records. But they still represent their country *together*."

He let his eyes move down the double line of people at the table. "They still have to support each other, root for each other, give each other courage." He leaned back in his chair. "So that's why I would like to see two people on *our* team decide to put an end to their quarrel right now. Come out of your corners, guys, and shake hands. Will you do that for me and the team?"

Donna started to get up. "I'm willing."

Doc turned to his right. "Crystal?"

"Sure, Doc," she answered, staring straight ahead rather than at either of them. "At the end of the meal."

"I don't get it," he said. "Why then?"

"I'm ... still digesting my food."

It was a stinging thing to say, and low murmurs rose up everywhere. "That's no answer, youngster."

"I'm not ready now."

"I'd like you to do it *now*."

"It wouldn't be honest, Doc. Do you want me to be dishonest?"

"Are you sure," he snapped, "that honesty is what we're dealing with here?"

Crystal was in no mood to reply, but she didn't have to.

Just then two waiters stepped out from behind the swinging doors of the kitchen carrying an enormous birthday cake, and the whole table burst into song.

Doc Stimpson's bushy eyebrows rose like two surfboards on a wave. "What's *this?* I told you it's not my birthday!"

"That's all right!" Dick Slocum, the assistant coach for the boys, called from the far end of the table. "We're going to pretend that it is!"

Stimpson threw up his hands. "Okay! Okay! You nailed me!"

"Hey, Doc!" one of the boys called. "We were afraid to put on enough candles because we didn't want you to get a heart attack trying to blow them all out!"

"I'll give *you* a heart attack if you don't watch out."

"Cut it out!" one of the other swimmers retorted. "Doc isn't that old. He's only ninety-eight."

"You kidding? That's his temperature! Doc is a hundred and fifty."

"No, birdbrain, that's how high his blood pressure goes when he sees you swim!"

"Okay! Okay! Anyone who has any more fun at my expense doesn't get cake."

There were loud protests that broke up into

more laughter and more jokes, which went on for the next fifteen minutes or so. Ellen leaned past Sabra. "Psst, Crystal. When is you-know-who coming?"

"You know that I'm a stickler for perfect timing," said Crystal out of the side of her mouth. She looked at her watch. "In just about sixty seconds."

Ellen leaned back and nudged the girl sitting next to her. She did the same to the one on the other side. Others who were scattered among the boys exchanged signaling glances too. Eyes turned carefully to the street door. And at the stroke of eight, in walked Bo Deaver.

One or two of the girls almost gasped. Hardly anyone had ever seen the easygoing basketball player in a blazer and pressed slacks before. He was as handsome as a movie star and seemed bigger than life as his long, graceful strides ate up the floor.

Ellen whispered feverishly into Crystal's ear, "Exactly on the dot. Wow! You sure know how to train your men!"

Crystal calmly brushed a few fallen crumbs from her billowing lace evening dress. There was nothing to do now but wait.

"Hi, gorgeous," he called when he was still fifteen feet or so away. "Ready to go?"

Crystal was taking her time as she started to rise, but he swept right past her ... and moved down the line to Donna's chair.

"Yes, you're a little early," said Donna. "But I guess so. Is that all right, Doc?"

"It's fine. Want a piece of cake, son?"

"Sure, if somebody will wrap it in a napkin. I finally found a taxi in this one-horse town, and it's waiting outside. Hi, Crystal, how you doing?"

Crystal didn't answer. Her face was bright red. And as Bo looked away Sabra whispered furiously in her ear, "I'll get even for you, Crystal! I swear I will!"

Meanwhile Bo had picked up the covered slice of birthday cake, and now he reached out to take Donna by the arm.

"Wait a minute." Stepping back from her chair, Donna walked down the line of swimmers to Crystal. She held out her hand. "Shake now?"

The eyes of every swimmer in the room were bearing down upon just one spot—and Crystal knew it. What she didn't know—and couldn't possibly believe—was that Donna had no idea in the world about what had been going on behind her back. Her *own* friends knew. *They* could all see. Crystal's humiliation was total. It swept over her like a roaring fire. And she couldn't bring herself to move.

Waiting there, truly having no idea about what was going on, Donna finally let her hand drop. Bo came up beside her and took her by the arm, leading her away. But her step was uncertain. When she reached the door of the restaurant, she stopped. The feeling that something was very wrong made her turn around.

She saw that Crystal was no longer in her seat but was fleeing—followed by several of her friends, led by Sabra—to the ladies' room.

* * *

On the way to the dance Bo explained to Donna what had happened. "I knew what she was up to," he said. "And I thought it was time someone taught her a lesson."

Donna had been listening very thoughtfully. "I'm sorry you did it, Bo. Why didn't you just stay away from her? Did you have to play games like that?"

Bo was hurt. "I just wish I could do something right with you, Donna."

"It *wasn't* right. How can I say that it was? And what I don't understand is you. You're such a gentle person. How . . . ?"

"I'm not that gentle. And I've told you before, I'm not that perfect." He was growing heated. "I'm tired of always being in the wrong, Donna."

"I haven't said you're always in the wrong."

"Well, I'm not as right as that Mr. Right back in Hick Town, New York, you're still mooning about!"

Donna gazed out the window at the dark outlines of trees. "I'm not enjoying this."

"Neither am I. Maybe we should just forget about the dance."

"Maybe we should."

"Hey, driver, pull over!"

"What are you doing?" she cried as he got out in the middle of a pitch-black mountain road, first handing the driver a few bills.

"What does it look like? Go on without me." A moment later he disappeared into the blackness. Donna got out and called after him several times, but there was no answer.

"What do you want me to do?" the driver patiently asked after a few minutes.

"We've got to find him."

"If he wanted to be found, he would have answered already." The driver started the car again, drove back to campus, and dropped her off at Evergreen Hall.

Donna was awake all night, twisting and turning endlessly. She went through her morning practice in a daze, but afterward she hurried through her stretches so that she would be early for Spanish class. If she could catch Bo before all the other kids came in, maybe there'd be enough time to apologize and make up with him. But Bo never showed.

Suddenly she had a horrible thought: What if Bo had not made it back to school at all? With her heart jumping to her mouth she searched the cafeteria for him at lunchtime. She went up to the table where the basketball players usually sat and asked if anyone had seen him. No one had. Bo had missed early-morning practice. She ran out of the building and headed for his dorm.

He wasn't in his room.

Frantically, not knowing where to look, she roamed the vast campus of Olympic High. But all the courts and tracks and practice areas were deserted now. She had searched everywhere but the corrals and stables. She passed them too. Then, all at once, Donna heard a loud snort and thundering hoofbeats. She turned and saw a wildly galloping horse headed right for her. The horse wore a bridle but no saddle. Sitting on its back, urging the animal on, was Bo Deaver.

Something about the sheer fury of the scene kept Donna from calling out. Suddenly the horse veered around and plunged at full speed straight for a low-lying fence. Although there were no stirrups to stand in, Bo rose up and seemed to lift the animal with him into the air. They cleared the fence with only a few inches to spare, then thundered on.

Then both Bo and the horse seemed to wind down. The animal slowed to an easy canter, then a trot, and finally to a cooling walk. Patting its neck and scratching its withers, Bo led the horse around toward the stables.

When he came outside again, Donna was standing a little distance off, waiting for him. Bo stopped, looked at her, and scratched his head. "Think I'll get in trouble for swiping Diablo and cutting everything? Haven't been on a horse since we sold ours and moved to Pittsburgh. Didn't know I was still any good at it."

Donna was trembling slightly. "I was afraid for you, Bo."

"Me? Why? I wasn't going to fall off."

"I mean . . . last night."

Bo shrugged. "I don't get into trouble on country roads."

"Oh, Bo, I'm so sorry about what happened." She wanted to run over and embrace him.

But there was something about the way he looked, a distance in his manner, that held her back.

"Listen," he said. "I've been thinking. Maybe we shouldn't see each other anymore. It's just too complicated."

"I . . . I don't understand."

"I think I'm just getting you more and more mixed up—and vice versa. Today is the first time I ever missed practice."

"I'm sorry, Bo."

"It's not your fault, but it's like I'm starting to act as though I don't even know what I'm doing anymore."

She stepped forward, reaching out to him. "Bo, can't we—"

"No, we *can't!* I tried to just be your friend, buddy-buddy, and all that, but it didn't work out." He managed to break into a little grin. "So, I'll still be a pal but at a little ways off, okay? I think that's for the best."

Donna felt the hot tears welling up in her eyes. But she fought them back. She also wanted to shout out loud, "Oh, Bo, I love you so." But what—what *stupid* thing prevented her from saying anything? Was it really Gregory? Or the fear of being hurt again? God, she was hurting right then so much!

Or was it Olympic High? Would Bo be one more tie to bind her here when she still didn't know . . . ?

"Hey," he said, wrapping an arm over her shoulder as they walked away. "Friends can love each other, right? Even ones who are gonna . . . keep a little space."

He kissed her cheek, and as he did, Donna's tears began to flow.

Chapter Ten

The swimming team was in the midst of its heaviest training for the big meet when Donna received an official-looking letter asking her to report to the dean's office. What could Dean Nolan want to see her about? She was doing okay in all of her classes, except maybe biology. She felt a momentary panic. She'd really botched a biology test the day after a run-in with Crystal at the pool. What if her grade had fallen below passing? She'd be suspended from swimming—and then how could she face Bret when he came out for the big meet?

Dean Nolan was watering the plants in her office when Donna rushed in. The moment the dean saw Donna, her face took on a grim cast. She set down the watering can, motioned Donna to a seat, and sat down behind her desk. Then, without a word, she handed Donna a computer printout of her grades. Donna read down the list. She stared disbelievingly at the *A* in biology.

"Is that accurate, Donna?"

Donna didn't know what to make of it. There was no way her biology grade could be an *A*.

"I don't understand this, Mrs. Nolan."

"Neither do we. Just in case of a computer error we always have our teachers double-check report cards after they have been printed out. Mr. Matthews said that he had given you a C– in biology."

"Well, the computer—"

"No, it wasn't a computer error. This was not the original grade that was fed into it. There is evidence that someone broke into the office at night and changed the grade."

"Mrs. Nolan, I—I wouldn't do that!"

"I can't believe that you would, either. But who else would have any reason to alter your grade? And you have had classes in computers, and I know you were worried about your biology grade."

"Yes, but—"

"Donna, this is so sad—and unnecessary. You'd pulled your biology grade up to a satisfactory level, anyway."

"Maybe . . . maybe it was just a mistake."

"I told you, it couldn't be a mistake."

"Then maybe somebody *wanted* to get me into trouble!"

"Who?"

"I don't know. *Yes!* Crystal Delehanty!" The dean stared at her disbelievingly, and Donna stumbled on. "Everyone thinks she's so wonderful. But she isn't! And she hates me! It has to be Crystal!"

"I don't believe that," the dean said softly. "I know her too well."

Donna was desperate. "Mrs. Nolan, you said

yourself that I didn't have any *reason* to do this!"

"All right, I'll send for her."

Fifteen long minutes later Crystal entered the office. She and Donna exchanged suspicious glances. "Something wrong, Mrs. Nolan?"

"Donna's biology grade has been tampered with to give her an *A* she didn't earn. She denies doing it. She says that someone must be trying to harm her. I know this is a terrible question to ask, but did you do this?"

Crystal's eyes blazed. "I certainly did not!"

Mrs. Nolan was clearly unhappy about pressing on, but she did. "Donna says that you have tried to do other bad things to her. Is that true?"

Crystal began to study the markings on the carpet at her feet. "She broke up a really important friendship of mine. So I tried to break up one of hers. But that was nothing like this. . . ."

A hopeful look was beginning to appear on the dean's face. Still she persisted. "We've narrowed down the time when it could have been done to Wednesday night between seven and eight-thirty. That's when the door was unlocked and the place was untended. Where were you then?"

Crystal folded her arms, lifted her head, and stared defiantly at both of them. "Where I always am at that time: at the pool, working out . . . with Doc Stimpson. Why don't you get him on the phone?"

"I don't have to. Thank you. You may go now."

Crystal strode out of the door, slamming it behind her.

"Well, Donna, that leaves us right back where we started, I'm afraid. Is there any further light you can shed on the matter?"

Donna was feeling hopeless. "No . . ."

Mrs. Nolan had a thought. "Is it possible," she asked softly, "that you did this for the *purpose* of being caught? So that you would have a reason for not staying on here?"

"No!" Donna cried out. "It is *not* possible!"

"I see. We will have to call a hearing to consider what action to take. You must realize how serious a charge this is. If you are found guilty, you could be suspended—or even expelled."

Donna fled the school building with only one thought—to find Bo. She ran as fast as she could toward the basketball courts. It was only when she piled up against the wire fence that she realized that it was raining hard. The players would be practicing indoors now. Besides, Bo wouldn't be able to leave practice, anyway.

She remembered, too, that they had agreed not to see each other for a while. But this was different, she told herself. He'd *want* to know! She'd wait outside the building until he came out. She'd tell him all about it. She'd cry. He'd take her in his arms. Somehow everything would be okay. . . .

But it wouldn't be. Bo would only get dragged into her problems again. Probably his coach was already giving him a hard time for cutting that practice session and for not keeping his mind on his game. Bo's future was at stake here too.

What about Bret? She'd tell Bret. Maybe he'd be able to do something. Wasn't he flying out in two weeks to see her swim? Maybe he could come earlier! She stumbled into the Student Center, which was the nearest building with a pay phone. "Operator, I want to put through a credit card call."

The next words never came out. A terrible cramp had gripped her stomach. The pain spread quickly and shot through to her back. Doubling over, she staggered to a sofa, then collapsed.

"What's wrong?" asked an elderly man, leaning over her. He was one of the school custodians.

Donna started to answer, but her teeth were chattering too violently. He put his hand onto her sweating forehead. "You're burning up! I'll get the doctor."

Twenty minutes later, she was lying in a bed in the school infirmary, glumly staring at the ceiling, feeling so depressed she didn't want to talk to anybody. "You'd better learn to take better care of yourself," said the physician, "and not stand around in the rain anymore. You were soaking wet when they brought you in here. Even at your tender age you could come down with something serious."

"I want to call my brother," she rasped.

He shook his head. "The thing you should do is rest and sleep." He smiled before leaving. "You're too young and too pretty to be letting yourself get run-down. Obviously something is troubling you, but that's no excuse to jeopardize your health."

Something? Is getting kicked out of school for cheating just *something?* she asked herself. Donna erupted into a bitter laugh that brought on another stab of pain.

Chapter Eleven

The news that Donna Wilder might be suspended for cheating hit Olympic High like a bombshell. Word raced through the school, and Bo heard about it the next day in Spanish class. "That's insane!" he exclaimed, and immediately went down to the dean to tell her so.

"I'm sorry, Bo. There's nothing I can do. We'll just have to wait for the hearing."

"Well, I'm going to find out who *really* did this!" he declared as he dashed out of the dean's office.

At lunchtime Bo walked from table to table in the cafeteria, asking if anyone knew who the head of the computer club was. Halfway through the period he found "Arms" Jameson, a huge weight lifter, sitting alone at a table in front of a mound of food.

"Listen," Bo said, swinging into a seat beside him. "I'm—"

"I know who you are. Seen you play. You ever watch me bench-press?"

"Not really."

"Don't worry about it. I'm the ace undiscovered athlete of this school. Except I don't think *anybody* knows who the discus thrower is. Do we have one?"

"Beats me."

The weight lifter took a gulp of food. "So what's happening, Captain?"

"My friend may get suspended for changing one of her grades."

"That was your girlfriend?"

"Yeah . . . well, a friend. I know she didn't do it, Arms."

"You know that, huh?" When Bo nodded, Jameson paused with his fork in midair and studied him carefully. "You never been fooled by a girl before?"

"That's not the kind of thing I'm talking about."

"No? Well, think about it."

"Hey, Arms," Bo said quietly, "don't put me on the spot. You're too big for me to hit. I'd break my hand."

"I know. I can get away with anything. It often makes me wonder why I waste my time being such a nice guy. All I can tell you, Judge, is that I didn't do it, either."

"Nobody's accusing you. I'm not accusing anybody."

"So how can I help you?"

"Do you know all the computer brains in this school?"

"The active ones, yeah. The other ones—how can I tell?"

"Okay. Do you have any swimmers in the club?"

"Swimmers?" Arms started to think.

"Crystal Delehanty?" Bo suggested eagerly.

"I only wish! You know her?"

"Sort of."

"You think you could get her to come and watch me curl a few hundred pounds?"

"I'd be the wrong one to ask her. Any of the other swimmers?"

"Not that I can think of. Maybe chlorine doesn't mix with silicon."

Bo rocked back in his chair and spread out his arms. "That shoots me down completely. I figure it *has* to be a swimmer."

Arms Jameson grew thoughtful. "There was this chick with long red hair who started with us a couple of years ago. But she had to drop out right away because of all her practicing."

Bo grew intense. "You remember her name?"

Arms shook his head. "No, but she's a baldy now. Goes around with a lace scarf over her head. See her around here all the time. Looks a little wacko. That any help?"

Bo was already on his feet. "Yeah!"

Lunch period was almost over, but Bo went looking for Sabra. He spotted her sitting at the swimmers' table. Ellen Navone was sitting next to her. The two of them had their heads down and were poring over some textbook together.

"See how this works, Sabra?" Ellen was asking.

"Oh, right! Now I get it."

Ellen gave her a hug. "You see? You were

just too clutched before. I think you're really beginning to come along now."

Sabra was just breaking into a smile when she saw Bo staring at her—and the smile froze on her face. Ellen, noticing that something was wrong, looked up too. But all she saw was Bo Deaver standing not far away, looking in their direction.

"What's the matter, Sabra?" she asked.

"Nothing!" Sabra hastily began gathering her books.

"The bell hasn't rung yet!"

"There's something I want to get. I have to do something."

Bo watched her go, then silently followed. There was a long passageway that connected the cafeteria to the school building. As soon as Sabra reached it she broke into a run. Bo only walked, but with his long legs, he kept pace with her. Sabra put on more speed. The swinging doors at the far end of the passageway were looming ahead of her now, almost within arm's reach. Suddenly her scarf came loose and fell to the floor. One of her hands flew to the top of her head. She couldn't go on without it. Turning back, she grabbed for the scarf, but Bo was already there, holding it in his hand.

"What are you bothering me for?" she practically screamed.

He fixed her with a stare. "Because I *know*."

"Know *what*? You're crazy! What are you talking about? *Leave me alone!*" She tore the scarf out of his hand and slammed through the swinging doors. Up ahead was one of the girls' washrooms. Sanctuary! Safety! She veered into it and did not leave until after the bell rang for the beginning of the next period. When she stepped back out into the hall, Bo was nowhere to be seen.

Sabra was a few minutes late getting to chemistry lab. Ordinarily that wouldn't have been a big deal. Today, however, the teacher was waiting with one of the makeup exams she would have to pass to get back to swimming.

She had studied hard for this one, and she was prepared. But she kept seeing Bo's face in her mind: What if somehow he really did know? She felt completely shaken. She tried to concentrate, but she couldn't. Finally the teacher came over to her. "Would you rather take this tomorrow?" he asked gently.

"Yes, Mr. Sullivan, please!"

"All right."

But it wasn't all right. When she left the lab, there was Bo Deaver, leaning against the hallway wall, his hands in his pockets, staring at her. She fled to her next classroom. During class break Bo reappeared again. This time at the window! She wanted to scream.

At the end of the school day she finally got away from him by slipping out of a side door and running across the campus. Safe! The basketball player couldn't possibly follow her around during his practice time.

And yet, when she was turning in a book at the library, she caught a momentary glimpse of him in the big mirror on the wall. That did it. She ran to her room in a panic and hid there, not daring to come out, even for supper. In the evening, when Crystal showed up to work with Sabra on one of her projects, she found her in a state.

"Something wrong? You flunk that exam again?"

"No, no. I'm going to take it tomorrow."

"I thought you were supposed to take it today. That's why we busted our brains over it."

"Yes, well I . . . he changed it. I guess there was something about the test. One of the questions." She stood up quickly, went to the window, and pulled the curtain aside. "Crystal, did you see anyone standing down there, looking up at the room?"

"Huh?"

"Never mind. Nothing."

"Listen, if there's some creep hanging around, let's notify security."

"No, no. I just . . . it was nothing."

"Sabra, what's going on?"

Sabra turned quickly. "I'm so glad we're friends again, you and I, Crystal."

"We never stopped being friends, as far as I know."

"Yes, but now it's different. We're helping each other. Not letting anybody— Nobody can hurt us anymore!"

"I really don't—"

"I was never jealous of you, Crystal! I mean, not really. I knew you were better than me. Far above me. That you were a star!"

"Come on, Sabra. What are you—"

"No, no, I mean it. This—what you're doing

here—is, is your destiny! But with me it's different. And I've accepted that. I don't mind that I have to work like a maniac for every little thing!"

"Believe me, I work for what I get too."

"But it's not the same! This is your fate! You were born for it! And I'm just so proud that I know you! And ... and that I'm your roommate! And I wouldn't let anybody hurt you!"

Something had begun to nag at the back of Crystal's mind.

"Are you, like, trying to tell me something, Sabra?"

A frightened look passed over the girl's face. "No, I just mean, *if* something would happen ... if anyone—"

Crystal persisted. "Was there ... something you did for me, Sabra?"

"No, Crystal, what do you mean?"

"Oh ... okay, never mind. You want to get to work now on your French? We can go over the vocabulary. Where's your book?"

"On the desk."

Crystal picked it up and began to open it. But all at once she closed it again with a bang. "Sabra, where were you about seven or eight on Wednesday night?"

"Where was I? I was studying with you."

"No, you weren't. I was still at evening practice then."

"Well, then, I don't remember." She shrugged. "I must have been doing something else."

"What?"

Sabra uttered a short, nervous laugh. "Really, do I have to report all my actions to you? You're not my mother, Crystal."

"I'm . . . I'm afraid to ask if you had something to do with what happened to Donna Wilder."

"Then don't ask!"

"You did it! You changed her grade to get her thrown out of school!"

"If I had done that—*if* I had done that, Crystal—how would you feel about it?"

"Terrible. I'd feel horrible!"

"Fine. Then you've got nothing to worry about. Because I didn't do it."

"Sabra, you remember what you said at the restaurant? That you were going to get even with her—or something!"

"Oh, *that* you remember. I didn't hear you saying anything to stop me *then!*"

"So you admit it!"

"I'm not admitting anything. This whole conversation is crazy! She changed her own grade!"

Crystal shook her head in disbelief. "No, I don't think so. Something's been telling me all day yesterday and today that she wouldn't do such a thing. She's just not the type to cheat."

"How come you suddenly think she's so great? It was *you*, wasn't it, who first said that she was the phony of all time? She broke up your friendship with Alex, then gloated over it! Look how she humiliated you at Doc's party!"

"I just know she's not a phony about her swimming. And why would you care about my friendship with Alex?"

"I care about somebody hurting you! You

said you wanted friends who are loyal. And I've proved that I'm loyal!"

"By doing something like this?"

Sabra broke into a stammer. "I-I didn't say I *did* anything. I just mean—"

"No. Wait a minute. No. You just said that you *proved* you were loyal. How did you prove it?"

"Look, Crystal, if you want to believe the worst of me, be my guest!"

"How did you prove it, Sabra?"

"End of discussion. End of all discussions. Forget about French!" She picked up the book and threw it against the wall. Then she leapt into bed and pulled the blanket up over her head.

"Come out from under there. I have to talk to you." But Sabra didn't answer. Crystal walked over to the bed and, reaching out gently, laid her hand on Sabra's shoulder. Sabra wrenched free and curled up into a tiny ball.

"Sabra," Crystal went on in a hushed tone, "please think about it. Look, it's not fair. I don't want to have anything to do with someone getting thrown out of school." She knelt beside the bed. "Listen, I don't like Donna Wilder, and it's true that she is a threat to me. But what do I get out of it if I beat her in a crooked way? Then I'm a loser too. Do you understand?"

Sabra's voice was muffled by her pillow. "I don't know why you're saying this to me. It's none of my business. I don't know anything about it."

"I don't think that's so. I think you made a very big mistake. And I want you to fix it."

"Don't you realize what will happen to *me* if I tell them what *you* think is the truth? I'll be the one they throw out of school."

"Maybe not. Not if you—"

Sabra turned to face her. "Who's lying now?" And when Crystal fell silent, she added, "Will you be the one who turns me in . . . friend?"

Donna spent one night in the infirmary, then she was sent back to the dorm. The doctor gave her some medicine that he said would calm her. Actually, it made her groggy. She pretty much slept the next day away, leaving her room only to go to the bathroom or to buy a few protein snack bars from the vending machine down in the basement. One time she awoke to find a note pinned to the door. Five words were written on it: "All is not lost! Bo."

That cheered her up, but it also made her very jumpy again. Her status was still up in the air. She couldn't deal with it. She felt the cramps returning and made her way back to bed. Two more days went by like that. There were more cheery notes from Bo, but he never knocked on her door. Never let her know he was there. She wondered a lot about that. Then the reason came to her. Bo didn't want to take advantage of the situation. He didn't want to hear her say something to him that came only out of gratitude. Dear, wonderful Bo. He never had asked for anything. How different from everyone else he was!

On the fifth evening someone did knock. It was Sabra Siebel! Her scarf off, her eyes staring, she looked as pale as a ghost.

"I'm the one," she said, "who did it to you. I must have been out of my mind. I'm sorry. Come on, let's go see the dean together."

Saying nothing, Donna tumbled into her clothes and walked with Sabra to the small private house where Mrs. Nolan lived. Sabra rang the bell and, when no one answered, rang again. Mrs. Nolan had been in the shower. "Can't this wait until tomorrow, Sabra?" she asked. But then she noticed Donna standing there too. Sabra almost didn't have to speak. Two and two were already being added up in Mrs. Nolan's mind by the time she led them into her house.

Chapter Twelve

Neither Donna's pleas nor those that Crystal made the next day were enough to keep Sabra in Olympic High. For a while Mrs. Nolan actually seemed to be reconsidering expelling her. But finally it was Sabra herself who made the decision to go.

"I've had my heart in my mouth as long as I've been here," she confessed to her roommate when they were alone together. "And it's turned me into a weirdo. First I was hurting myself, then I ended up hurting other people too."

Crystal seemed even more downcast than Sabra. "And me—I was so tied up with being the Golden Girl that I let you down."

"No, you didn't. What did you owe me? You had your own life to think about, that's all."

Sabra's words didn't satisfy Crystal. "I should have tried harder to help you."

"You can do it now. Promise to keep in touch with me."

"You got it!"

"And promise to keep winning!"

Crystal backed off slightly. "There's only one

person I make that promise to, Sabra. Me. Otherwise I'd get very uptight."

Sabra grinned. "Okay. Forget that one."

"Can I help you pack?"

"Sure. And there are some things I want to give you. Starting with *this*." She pulled the Spanish lace scarf off her head and handed it to Crystal.

Then they both began to cry.

Donna couldn't quite believe that the cloud of suspicion over her had been lifted as quickly as it had fallen. For some minutes nothing seemed real to her, not even Sabra's account of how Crystal had pressed her to tell the truth—and what Bo had done to shake her up.

Bo!

She went flying to the Student Center. She found him in the study room, sitting behind his usual pile of books. She didn't have to say a word. The moment he saw her radiant face, he knew. He jumped up from his chair, glowing.

But something happened in the split second it took before she flew into his arms. He seemed to draw back.

"Bo," she pleaded, "you've done so much for me. Please don't pull away from me now."

"Listen, that's the last thing I want to do. But I need to know where we stand."

Her eyes were glistening. "I don't think I care about Gregory anymore."

"You don't *think*—or you know?"

"B-Bo," she stammered. "I'm so confused about everything right now. I don't *know* about anything. Can't you just give me a little time?"

He took her hands in his for just a moment and smiled faintly. "I guess I really don't have too much choice, do I? I haven't been all that successful at keeping at a distance from you."

She looked up at him with soulful eyes. "Please don't sound so worried, Bo. Do you think I'd ever hurt you?"

"I'll tell you what I think," he said, trying to change the subject. "That swimming meet with San Diego is coming up. I really hope you're going to sit it out."

"Why?"

"Because you've been sick. You've been under a lot of strain. Look at yourself—you're completely drained."

"Bo, I'm fine. I really am. And my brother is coming to see me swim."

"You're not fine—and you should tell him not to come."

"I can't do that. He's counting on it."

"Then tell him *not* to count on it! That's just the problem, don't you see?"

"You don't understand," she said dejectedly.

Bo took her by the arm. "Listen. Do *you* want to swim in that race? You? For yourself?"

"I don't know! I just can't think about it!"

"Then there's something *you* need to understand. There are times to show everybody what you can do. And there are other times to just go walking up a trail, put your feet in a stream ... maybe do a little fishing ... get to know yourself."

"I've never been fishing," she said shyly. "Would you teach me?"

"You bet! Let's make a deal. You pass on the meet and I'll take you fishing and riding and even, Heaven forbid, for a swim. I know a great spot. It's right under a waterfall!"

"Bo," she said. "Can't we do that afterward? I've got to get back in shape for my events on Saturday. I'm here to *compete*."

"Yeah, Donna—but for whom?"

"You sound," she blurted out, "just like Gregory!"

"Okay, then ask yourself: How did things go with him?"

Donna knew that he was making some kind of a point. But she didn't want to think about it. What she needed now, she told herself, was a little space.

When in doubt about anything, Donna had always plunged into a pool. This was what she'd intended to do as soon as practice started again the next morning.

But when the time came, before she could jump into the water, all the other swimmers came rushing over to pat her on the shoulders, hug her, welcome her back! Then, wonder of wonders, Crystal stepped forward, holding out her hand.

Donna took it in silence. Nothing had to be said. Crystal turned and dove into the pool. Then all the other kids—Donna included—jumped in after her. Bobbing, turning, thrashing around, Donna was definitely sure of one thing: the water felt good. And there was something else that felt good too: being accepted.

"Just take it easy," Jim Sileki called to her after twenty minutes or so of warm-ups and general fooling around. "You look worn-out. Don't push yourself. I don't think we're going to use you in this meet."

Donna felt a momentary surge of relief. And then she had a vision of Bret sitting on the sidelines. On his face was that same look he'd worn that day when Dr. Weingarten called to give the family the news that his swimming career was over.

"Jim," she called out, "I *am* going to be in it!"

"Then you'll have to show me you're in condition."

"I *will* show you!" she cried. But then swimming became work again. And ten minutes later she began to feel the stomach cramps returning.

In the days that followed Donna hid from everyone the pain and nausea that kept sweeping over her in waves. Nor did she say a word about the nightmare—the same one—which kept repeating itself in more and more detail as the contest grew nearer. She would awake in the middle of the night and sit on the edge of her bed for hours, afraid to go back to sleep.

But in the daytime she refused to spare herself at practice. She, herself, began to wonder about what she was doing. Wasn't this some kind of madness? Would Bret really want to see her torture herself just for one meet? Why didn't she just call him on the phone before he left Platterkill and ask him not to come?

Why was she *doing* this to herself?

All the clamoring in her head changed nothing. It had no effect at all on the physical Donna, who had control of her body and was driving it on with the kind of fury only Sabra could have matched.

The week passed, and on Friday she got the message that her brother had reached Denver and was already on the bus to Olympic High. And just as her classes came to an end, there he was! He met her right outside the school building, crying, "Hi, Do-Do!" Then he swept her into the air, as if she were still the little girl he used to call by that name.

"Hi, Bret!" She threw her arms around his neck. She loved him so.

"You got to go to afternoon practice?" he asked, setting her down.

"No, they've cut it so we can all rest up for tomorrow."

"Great! Then we can just spend some time together."

"Where are your bags?"

"I only have an overnight. I left it at the guest house. Some fabulous setup you've got here! Come on, show me around."

"I'd love to."

"Wait a minute. Let me get another look at you." He studied her for a while. "You're looking a little worn-out, kid. You sure you're all right?"

"Of course. Everything's great!"

"Positive?"

"Uh-huh. Yes." Oh, why couldn't she tell

him the truth? The truth—what was the truth, anyway? "Oh, Bret, Bret, I'm so glad to see you!"

As she said the words she knew how much she meant them. Her brother was here! And she leaned her head on his shoulder as they walked across the grounds of Olympic High.

Donna barely slept that night. Maybe she didn't want the nightmare to come again. She was still feeling groggy and exhausted when she showed up at the swimming building in the morning. Suddenly she was frightened as well. Looking around at the visiting team during warm-ups, Donna recognized more than a few faces from the covers of swimming magazines. It began to hit her that this was more than a tough team; some of these people were already champions!

As she tried to push away the fear it was replaced by a kind of spreading numbness. When the first race began—a relay—she looked on in a haze, barely noticing when San Diego won it hands-down. She wasn't even aware that Jim was speaking to her until he repeated himself. "Sorry, Donna, but I can tell you're not up to it today. I'm not putting you in any of the races."

"You can't do that!" she shouted at him, though he was only inches away. "I've got to swim, Jim. I've *got* to!"

"You're really crazy, you know that? I can see that something's dragging you down. And I'm not going to—"

"You're wrong," she cut in with a nervous little laugh. "I'm just kind of hyper now, you know? This is a big day for me."

"Okay," he said, only half convinced. "You'll do your best event—the two-hundred freestyle—but that's it. It's you, Crystal, and Ellen, for us. And I think you ought to know that one of the girls swimming against you is Doris Halley."

"Who?"

"You've got to be kidding. You never heard of her? She was national record holder two years ago."

"Oh, right." Donna remembered her now. It was just that the numb feeling was getting in the way of everything, including her thinking.

Just then she heard the announcement for the women to take their places on the blocks. It was her event.

"If you're going to go, go!" Jim said quickly. "Take lane two."

Even in her daze Donna realized that she was not considered the fastest swimmer in this event; lanes three and four were reserved for the girls with the fastest times so far—Crystal and Doris Halley. She glanced at the benches that had been set up along the sides of the pool. Bret was there, and the expression on his face said, "Show them, kid! Show them all!"

She felt the panic breaking through her grogginess. And suddenly the starter's gun seemed to go off, not at poolside, but in her own head.

Donna had no clear sense that she was jumping now, that she had hit the water, that her arms were lashing out. She wasn't even sure what got her down the length of the pool and into her turn. But all at once, as she was nearing the middle of the second lap, things began to happen just as they had so many times in her nightmare.

Only now it was much more vivid. Now she could hear the cries of the spectators. Now she could see her brother's face turn completely to the color of ashes. Now she could feel the pain spreading in her stomach and flooding through her limbs. She could feel herself losing all control, her body becoming like a stone.

There was nothing she could do to keep her head from going completely under!

The water encircled her face. She could not rise, could not breathe. She kept thinking, *Bret will come for me! Come for me!*

Bret became Bo. Then Bo became Bret. But no one came! She could not cry out. Could not hold back the water from her lungs. Donna gasped for air. But it was water—water—water—drowning water that entered...

Choking and sputtering, Donna jerked upright in bed. Somehow the bedclothes had gotten tangled over her head. It had been a dream. Only a dream!

Donna's whole body trembled as she pushed off the bed. She had to feel her way out of the room. She staggered down the hall as though she were drunk. And, reaching the bathroom sink, she heaved up whatever was left in her stomach, as if it were the water of the pool.

Several hours later it was time for the real meet. Donna was the last to arrive. Her teammates were all there. So were the swimmers from San Diego. Her brother was sitting among the spectators on the portable benches. Bo was in the crowd too. Both of them sent her signals of encouragement. But there was something else in Bo's eyes—a look of real concern.

Then, exactly as in the nightmare, Jim Sileki began the same conversation with her. Inwardly Donna shuddered, but she found herself uttering the same replies, as if it were her fate to go out there—and die.

When the announcement came, she took her place on the block at lane two. "Swimmers take your marks!" the starter said. She went into her crouch. And at that moment—the moment when she knew what she was facing—Donna made her decision.

This race, she told herself, is for Bret. But it's my last one ever. A feeling of warmth swept over her body. Her stomach began to unknot. And the starting gun went off.

This was Donna's farewell swim, and she put everything she had into it. There were those among the spectators who later said it was as if they were watching a dance, someone moving to music. In perfect, graceful rhythm her arms and legs glided like the limbs of a sea creature. It was hard to believe she was racing, and yet Crystal, for all her finishing power, could not keep up with her. Doris Halley, the tested champion, fought with everything she had to take the lead. But Donna swept to the finish half a body length ahead of them both.

The crowd was electrified. In their separate

places Bo and Bret stood up to cheer. Crystal, shaking off her own disappointment, came over to embrace Donna. Doc Stimpson's proud face swam into view along with Sileki's. They were both saying something about a new record.

Then suddenly someone was crying, "Catch her!"

A feeling that had started as a tingling in her feet became a blinding dizziness as it rose to her head. She took a half turn, uttered a little cry, and dropped to the deck.

Bo Deaver stood outside the infirmary, pacing back and forth.

"Who are you?" Bret, who was also waiting, finally asked. "And why are you glaring at me like that?"

Bo immediately stopped, came over, and barked in his face. "I hope you're satisfied now!"

"What's your problem, buddy?"

"You! You're the so-called *brother* who drove her to this!"

"You want to stop spraying me with your saliva and tell me what you're *talking* about?"

"I don't believe this. Such ignorance!"

"What—"

Just then the doctor came out. "You can relax, Mr. Wilder. She's been under a lot of stress—for a long time, apparently—but she's going to be all right."

"Can I go inside?" Bo asked anxiously.

"Sure. You both can."

"No," said Bret, pushing past them. "First the terrible ogre wants to find out what's going on."

* * *

Donna was awake and looking alert but very tired. "You sure know how to scare the heck out of a brother," he said, kissing her on the forehead.

"I'm sorry, Bret. I guess it was all the . . . the pressure."

"There's some flagpole outside who seems to think that I'm responsible for all this."

She sat up. "Bo? Is Bo there?"

"If he looks ten feet tall, that's him."

"Can I see him?"

"Talk to me first." He took Donna's hands and pressed them. "Tell me, *was* it me? Did I somehow push you too hard? Because I never meant to, you know."

"Bret, Bret—I don't want to race anymore."

Bret walked over to the window and stared out at the vast sweep of Olympic High for a few minutes. Then he turned to face his sister.

"Okay, so you don't want to race. No big deal."

She gazed at him in amazement. "You don't mind?"

It was his turn to be surprised. He paused only slightly. "What have I got to do with it? That's up to you, isn't it?"

"But, Bret, it means so much to you, doesn't it?"

He walked back to her bedside. "Well, sure. Right. I'm as proud as I can be of my kid sister. I love to see you strutting your stuff. But, Do-Do, I'd be just as proud of you—and I'd love you just as much—if you were still hanging out at the soda fountain back in Platterkill. What's that got to do with anything?"

Now she was completely confused. "Didn't ... didn't you want me to go to the Olympics?"

"Yeah, sure. If that's what *you* want. I thought you fell in love with the idea when you saw me trying for it. I was just trying to give you encouragement." He walked to the window again, looked out, and turned around abruptly. "Donna, did you get the idea, somehow, that I was trying to make you—uh—take my place or something?"

"Uh . . ." The silence she fell into said it all.

"I don't believe this! Are you trying to tell me you came here to this school because of me?" She nodded. "And yesterday, when I thought you weren't looking so hot, you were really sick then?"

"Sort of . . ."

"So, in some way, you pushed yourself through this race because of me?"

Tears came into Donna's eyes as she nodded.

"I just don't get it. What would make you think you owed this to me?"

"Because," she cried, "it was my fault!"

"*What* was your fault?"

"The accident that stopped you from swimming!"

"Hey, nutcake! How did you ever get that idea?"

"Because . . . because I asked you to drive faster that day when you were taking me to the movies. Then you skidded on the ice and we went into that stupid embankment. And that's when you ruined your knee!"

"This is incredible! You were only seven years old when that happened. I messed up my knee long after that, a couple of years ago—"

"I know! But Dr. Weingarten said that the accident was how it started. And it got aggravated again when—"

"Yeah," he broke in, "when I was dumb enough to go out and play touch football. Some idiot decided to break the rules and tackle me, and I went crashing down on the hard pavement."

"But I caused the accident that *started* it!"

"What started it was that I didn't have enough sense to put on my seat belt—that's what started it. And I didn't drive any faster just because you asked me to. It was just bad luck. I simply hit a patch of ice. That was all." He started to grin. "But, listen, if you want to take the blame for my stupidity, be my guest. And if you want to go out and win a lot of prizes just so you can give them to me, that's okay too. And, listen, later on, if you feel like making a million bucks that I can help you spend—"

"Okay! Okay! I get it." She was smiling now too.

He marched to the door. "So say good-bye to your new boyfriend and arrange how you're going to have him come out and visit us back home. I'm going to see the powers-that-be at Olympic High and pack you up. You're coming home with me to Platterkill!"

Chapter Thirteen

Donna's return home was very quiet. Her parents greeted her almost as if she were a wounded soldier coming back from the war. They spoke softly, wrapped her in love, and set her down between clean sheets in her own room. In a way that made her smile, for Donna was perfectly well by now. Still, she said nothing to stop them. This protectiveness really fit right into a need she felt to have everything in her life—from her movements to her thoughts—slow way, way down.

Imagine! she thought, lying back on her pillow in the middle of the day and idly gazing at a window curtain billowing in the breeze. No more mad dashes from practice to classes to practice to study to sleep! No day-in and day-out dangling from kickboards, pounding away. No stretches, warm-ups, endless laps. No worrying about Crystal Delehanty's stroke.

But no more Bo Deaver, either. She heaved a very heavy sigh and, getting slowly off the bed, went to the special cabinet where, since earliest childhood, she had kept her growing collection of dolls. She looked at them, one by one.

The first day or so, Donna stayed close to the house, puttering about in her room, helping her mother bake, just lingering around, feeling safe. Then, when she felt ready to deal with the high energy of her friends—and all the questions they were certain to ask—she began making a few calls.

They bubbled all over her, and soon she was out with this one or that one hitting the shopping malls, taking in movies, gossiping—and having a lot of fun. Then one afternoon she spotted Gregory driving by in a car with one of his cousins. She barely exchanged quick glances with him, but later that night he called.

"Hi Donna."

"Hi. How are you?"

"Pretty good." There was a silence. "I hear that you . . . uh . . . that you're coming back to school here."

Hearing Greg on the other end of the line somehow made her yearn for the sound of a different voice. An image of the tall, gentle basketball player she'd left behind in Colorado floated before her mind. It gave her a deep, deep pang. But she was still on the phone with Gregory, and he was waiting for an answer. "I guess so," she replied vaguely, no longer quite recalling what they were talking about.

Now Gregory seemed confused. "I . . . I thought they said you were back for good."

She gave a forced little laugh. "Well, I am, so I'd better go to school, right? Or else I'll be a juvenile delinquent and they'll send me off to the prison farm or something!"

"Yeah, right!" He seemed happy to hear her laugh. But then his own tone began to sink. "I . . . guess you're feeling really down on me after my letter and all."

Gregory's letter? She almost had to remind herself about that. It seemed like something that had made her unhappy once—years and years ago. But what did that have to do with now? "No, Greg," she answered. "I don't blame you for anything at all."

"You don't think I was a rat?"

"No, why should I? I was the one who left." She paused for a moment, then added, "And at least you were straight with me, Greg. You didn't go out with someone first, behind my back. I appreciate that." She broke off. Heavy feelings were starting to come back to her. She didn't want to deal with them or even find out what they were. She still needed to keep everything *light*.

"You know," Greg was saying in an embarrassed manner, "I've had a few dates, but I really haven't been seeing anyone. And I still—"

"Greg," she interrupted quickly, "I'm just not into—"

"Hey!" he cut back in, "I'm not talking about our going together again. I'm only—"

"Please, Greg. Let me finish. I was about to say that I don't want to talk about serious personal things. You kids in Platterkill have had a summer vacation, but I haven't had any.

Right now I just want to see my friends and relax. That's all I want."

"Any ... any reason why I can't fit into that 'friend' part? I mean ... uh ... I was just wondering if you wanted to take a bike ride with me tomorrow? We could go out to Echo Lake, maybe do some canoeing...."

"I don't know, Greg."

"Hey, don't worry. No touching. Just talking and getting to know each other again. Okay?"

"Fine," Donna answered, as if she suddenly felt good about the idea. But she wasn't at all so sure after she hung up. And what, she asked herself as an image of Bo Deaver—dearest, dearest Bo!—swam before her mind, had she agreed to do it for?

Gregory came over on his bike the next morning carrying a little backpack full of picnic food. "All set?"

Donna nodded, pumped a little air into her front tire, and they set off. They rode along, pretty much in silence, with Gregory more or less leading the way. She wondered if biking would keep her swimming muscles in shape. Not that it mattered anymore, of course. Their path took them away from main highways and down one of the tree-lined streets that led to the outskirts of town.

Then they turned onto a country road that Greg knew she had always loved. Donna stared beyond it to the low-lying hills in the background—and before her mind suddenly flashed a picture of the towering ring of peaks circling

Olympic High. "Do you know there's snow on one of them?" she found herself saying aloud.

"One of *what?*"

"Mountains . . . there's snow on one of the mountains in Colorado. Even in summer."

Now they were passing the estates of the super-wealthy. And up ahead, behind a long stone fence, loomed the huge private swimming pool of the family that owned a good half of Platterkill. As usual, there was absolutely no one using it.

What a waste! she told herself, staring at the glittering green water. By this hour, back at Olympic High, the swimmers would be crowding into the water for morning practice. Crystal was probably leading them off right now in the repeats practice. She'd be doing it in all the strokes now that Donna wasn't there to share the lead-off honors.

Passing the pool, Donna coasted the bike and circled back for another look. A slow smile began to spread across her face as her imagination conjured up a race between just the two of them, her and Crystal Delehanty, the Golden Girl. But she, too, was a Golden Girl now as their arms, covered with droplets, looking like jewels, rose and plunged into the water, again and again. Would Crystal win? Would she? Or would they tie as they so often did? In a way it mattered. And in a way it didn't. Goose bumps were rising up her back.

"I beat her the very first day!" Donna exclaimed aloud. And once again a bewildered

Gregory had to ask her what she was talking about.

Donna turned to stare at her old boyfriend, realizing that she really didn't want to answer him. Or rather, it didn't matter whether she did or not. He was not the person she wanted—absolutely *needed*—to share things with. Tears formed in the corners of her eyes.

Bo again.

More separate than together, Donna and Gregory pedaled along in a silence that must have been very wearing on him. "Look," he said at last, pulling over to the side of the road. "This isn't really working. I just don't feel that you're really here with me."

She lowered her eyes. "You're right—and I'm sorry."

"What gets me is that I'm not trying to push you into anything. I haven't put any pressure on you, have I?"

"No, Greg," she admitted. "You've been very nice."

"Only you really can't forgive me, right?"

"It isn't that."

He took a deep breath. "There's somebody else."

She nodded.

Greg forced a thin grin. "Pretty terrific guy, huh?"

"Yes . . ."

"Great athlete, I suppose. Not like me."

She gazed directly at him. "That has nothing to do with it."

"Okay," he said softly. "It's none of my business, anyway. I'm glad you found somebody you like."

"Thank you."

"And being a friend now instead of a boyfriend, I'd kinda like you to tell me about him."

"Are you sure you want me to?"

"Yeah." He sighed.

"Well, he's very kind . . . and gentle. And he has a wonderful sense of humor. And most of all," she went on, growing more excited, "a way of knowing when you're feeling—"

Gregory held up his hand in a little signal to stop. "Listen, I know I asked you, but I . . . uh . . . when I see your eyes lighting up like that for some other guy, then I guess I'm not really ready. I mean, I still feel something and I—" He looked away.

"This was a good meeting, Greg," she said slowly. "I guess we had to have it. To sort of bring things to a certain place, I mean."

"Yeah, I guess so."

"I'm sorry it had to be painful."

"Hey, listen. That's the name of the game, getting together, breaking up—right?"

"I hope we really can be what we said—friends."

"Yeah, sure. Down the line we will." He paused. "I think I gotta find somebody first, you know?"

"I sure do."

He gazed up at her with a warm smile. "Well, do we go on with this ride or do we shake hands?"

"I think we shake hands." She smiled back.

"Well, see you later." He swung back onto his bike and rode on ahead.

She watched him go, then turning around, headed off toward home. Perhaps it was more than just an impulse that led her to take a change of direction. She wasn't really thinking about it, but after a series of turns, she found herself spinning along the service road to Platterkill High.

The old school was spread out in one long, low line—a drab, single-story brick building that now reminded her of a factory. Donna hadn't always felt that way about it. She'd had many good—as well as a few bad—times in this place. Now she turned onto the path that led past the ball fields to curve around behind the gym.

She stopped and gazed at it all. What would life be like for her here now? she asked herself. Would she join the Platterkill swim team after she had raced for Olympic High? Or would she just do her schoolwork and hang out the rest of the time? Hanging out—was that what she did best? And who would she be sharing her feelings with?

She was being a little unfair to herself, of course. There were friends here, old friends, who wanted to know what was going on inside of her. But how could she explain what it was like to go into a race while she was doubled over with cramps and go on to break a record? Or the heartbreak she felt for poor Sabra, who had tried to have her thrown out of school?

And who could listen half as well as that tall, tall, tall basketball player with the slightly cockeyed grin?

Bo Deaver received a letter. "Dearest," it said. "It's you—just you. No one but you. You! You! You!" That's all the letter said. Nothing more.

Two weeks after that, Crystal Delehanty got a letter too. "Hold on to your times! I'm coming back!"

Crystal stopped by the basketball court to show it to Bo. "What do you make of it?"

"Competition returneth!"

She studied his face. "I think love returneth too." From brow to chin and ear to ear, Bo Deaver was beaming like the sun itself.